THE PRIME MINISTER'S SON

ROGER BLOUNT

The Prime Minister's Son
Published by The Conrad Press Ltd. in the United Kingdom 2025

Tel: +44(0)1227 472 874
www.theconradpress.com
info@theconradpress.com

ISBN: 978-1-917673-13-6

Copyright © Roger Blount, 2025

All rights reserved.

Typesetting and Cover Design by: James Sadlier, jamessadlier@me.com
The Conrad Press logo was designed by Maria Priestley.

Printed and bound in Great Britain by Clays Ltd, Elcograf S.p.A

There is a fine line between:

'Should the people control the State or should the State control the people'.

It is perilous to step too far to the wrong side of that line.

CHAPTER ONE
OH, MY PAPA!

'No!'

The single syllable roared across the room, hit the far wall and fragmented into silence. In the centre of the room, Marcus felt the word sweep over him like a wave but he was unmoved. As a child, he remembered the many times his father roared at him in a similar fashion and he would step back, overpowered by the force of the volume and the threat it carried and the furniture would withdraw to the walls leaving him to drown in an ocean of carpet; but now Marcus only felt a deep contempt rising inside him. His father had turned away, filling the window area with his huge frame and casting gloom into the room.

The Prime Minister finally turned and waved one hand with agitation. 'Can't you see they are playing you like a fish on a hook just to get at me?'

'Why does it always have to be you?'

The Prime Minister stepped closer to his son but Marcus was now the taller and his closeness posed no awe. 'It is because I am the Prime Minister. They are baiting you to catch me. Any fool could see that.'

'But I am not a fool.' Marcus countered, 'I know what they want and why they are doing it.' He paused for effect, 'And Father, I am willing. I want to do this.'

The Prime Minister turned away quickly and moved across the room and sat down behind his desk; to him it was an extension of his authority but to Marcus it was just another barrier. His voice became quiet, almost to a hush. 'I am your father. Is this some sort of vengeance for something I have done?'

Marcus broached the barrier by leaning forward and placing his hands flat on the desk. 'No. It is for things you have not done. Have never done. You were not there at my birth. An important union meeting I think you told my mother. I was two days old before you managed to visit us. And even more incredulous, you were not there at mother's death.'

The Prime Minister jerked his chin forward. 'I did not know. They did not warn me her death was imminent.'

'Her health had been failing for a week. Death did not set itself by your clock.'

The Prime Minister's face flushed a brighter red; he traced his mind back to that time. His son had been eight years old when his wife had died and he had not realised he had sown a seed and his son quietly harboured a grudge; a growing hatred in his mind. He felt he had done the best by him; arranging for Marcus to board at the best school available. 'I did what I thought best for you.'

Marcus read his mind. 'Oh yes. You packed me off to a wonderful school that cost a fortune. It was a great opportunity for the boy while you basked in the sympathy of your acolytes.'

'It seemed to have done you some good,' the Prime Minister demurred. 'Until now,' he added.

Marcus stood upright. 'How would you have known? You were never there. You were never there to collect me at end of term; you always sent a car. And then there was the annual prize giving. Oh yes. Did you know I won prizes for sport and for academic achievements?'

'Of course I did. I kept in touch.'

'You mean your secretary passed you notes. Do you know she often rang me? We used to have long conversations. She was just like a mother; always full of excuses for you. And then when I went to university; I heard you crowing to your union pals; "Marcus will make something of himself; but hopefully not a politician." And they all laughed obediently.'

The Prime Minister had had enough and he stood up. He went around the desk and faced his son closely but the usual effect of his large presence failed again to dominate. The Prime Minister, finding he had to look up to his son, turned and walked away. He paused again by the window; sighed and slowly turned. 'You realise the damage this could do to me. Not me personally but what I stand for. I am not....'

But Marcus interrupted him. 'I realise precisely what you stand for and that is why I am doing this. I came here as a curtesy to tell you myself before you read it in the newspapers, but I see I have wasted my time.' He turned and went to the door where he paused and looked back. 'You think that all things revolve around you and that is why I want to bring you down. Well, you are right in that respect. I do want to bring you down just for mother's sake.' He opened the door and was gone before his father could say anything

The Prime Minister looked at the closed door; he thought not about the apparent loss of a son but more, his parting words. Times were difficult enough but now his son could add a whole new dimension to his problems. He went over to his desk, took out a key from his pocket and unlocked the top, left drawer. He took out a mobile phone and pressed a button; it only had one dialling number stored. He waited and had only a few seconds before a voice, deep and precise, simply acknowledged the call.

'Ten-o-clock tonight; at the usual place,' the Prime Minister said.

'Very good,' was the simple response and the 'phone went dead.

He had just locked the 'phone away again when

there was a knock at the door and his Secretary looked in the room. 'You have a meeting with the Home Secretary and the Chancellor. Do you want to see them here?'

The Prime Minister nodded. 'And don't bother with any tea, Gerald. I need to keep it short.'

Gerald smiled, disappeared for a moment and then the two men entered. He followed them in and arranged two chairs in front of the desk and then left without a word.

The Prime Minister sat down and waved them to the chairs. 'Well, what could possibly have gone so wrong that both of you need to see me so urgently and together?' He began to chuckle to lighten the mood. 'I mean, who is running the country if all three of us are here?'

'I'm glad you find it so amusing, John,' the Chancellor Archie MacDonald said with his usual stoical voice, heavily laden with his Scottish accent.

Toby Fennel, the Home Secretary grinned with mirth; he not only found what the PM had said amusing but also that the Chancellor had not. Over the past few months, the relationship between himself and the Chancellor had become strained over their diverging views. He saw the Chancellor as a 'bean counter' with no imagination and with bony claws which clung on to every penny without a triplicate justification.

What had started as a grand 'new beginning' for the government had first frayed around the edges of the political parachute and was now, over the last few years, threatening to shred into a free fall. The Daily Mail had recently dubbed them: 'The Three Moscowteers'. MacDonald was pleased with it but Fennel felt it was more ominous. Any tag associating them with Moscow would alienate a good portion of the public and relationship with the US was strained enough. He remembered the Foreign Secretary had turned a deep purple when he heard of it.

'So,' the Prime Minister interrupted both their thoughts. 'What is it you want?' He looked at MacDonald as he asked the question.

'Time,' MacDonald was as usual, succinct and saved words like coins. 'John, we always knew that our economic plan would need time to… to mature. Aye, mature.'

The Prime Minister, John McVey, noted the Chancellor used his first name; he always did when he wanted him on his side, especially against the Home Secretary. Time, he thought, what a small word but how potent. Theresa May had played with time to get her obstinate way but time had eroded her pedestal of power; Jeremy Corbyn had waited for the right time but his procrastination had been seen as a weakness and time had hastened before him. Someone had labelled Jeremy Corbyn the 'opportunist mugwump'; and while this was a contradictory phrase, the meaning struck home and sunk his hopes of leadership.

Boris Johnson had used time to set ambitious targets and make promises but missed each one over Brexit and then the Covid-19 Pandemic and topped it all with 'Partygate' as the Press had dubbed it. And so, after a time, he had lost his credibility. Truss was a five minute disaster and eventually, Sunak took the reins but his quieter approach implied weakness to some and simply paved the way for a change of government when he called for an election against advice.

Although Labour had a new leader whose quiet demeanour had offered promise of a new way, the devastating worldwide effects of the Pandemic bit more deeply and it was greatly aggravated by the Ukraine war and both main parties began to implode.

First Truss and then Sunak fuelled the inner fighting of the Conservatives which tore them apart and Labour had not the strong leadership to take immediate advantage. The economy plummeted and strikes threatened to echo the seventies decade of Union power and as the next set of elections loomed the Liberal Democrats were failing again to offer their selves as a credible alternative and the possibility of a period of an unworkable majority or a hung parliament was looming.

Labour was the obvious alternative and to the chagrin of the right who hoped the Tories might just hang on; Farage opened old wounds and sowed more doubt. They overturned the large Tory majority with a landside advantage, but a strong leadership was a nagging problem and Labour, so long the critic was now seen floundering against a growing tide of public expectancy. Their problems were recovering from the Conservative legacy finding the coffers not only empty but steeped in hidden debts. They had mastered sniping from the bushes but it was another matter to stand in the full glare of public and media spotlights.

John McVey had bided his time until the next election drew near and then he stepped in with powerful speeches and a promise he had a plan to repair the crumbling edifice of what could loosely be called a self-destructing Parliament and with his powerful presence and oratory, had rejuvenated the image of the Labour Party and offered a strong alternative. He offered a unification of the Labour party with the people and the phrase: 'Bottom up Economics'. By directing funding through the lower classes with opportunities for major rebuilding projects with the renationalisation of water, rail, power and with higher spending for roads and housing, but in a carefully scheduled way over ten years, he promised rejuvenation of the economy for the working classes without punitive measures to the rich. McVey insisted that his manifesto would allow him to manage to rebuild the country after the years of post-Brexit inertia followed by a further two years of trying to unpick the EU strands which held fast like the Gordian knot and the wilderness in the aftermath of the Pandemic and subsequent confusion, with no party offering viable and serious solutions, the weary populous saw this as the only option.

The people and economy were weary and desolated after Brexit and the Covid-19 Pandemic and most politicians, mindful of their own careers and positions, drew back and allowed the boisterous and sometimes bullying tactics of McVey to prove succour to the millions who were distraught of a way back to better times and McVey also convinced his own party and was elected as the new leader and surprised everyone by calling for a snap election.

McVey stormed to a manageable majority and at first his plans and dreams had worked, as new things tend to do before they are put to the test but time, that entity that sits closest to death, began to unpick the strands of visions.

McVey had swept into power given gratefully by a population wearied by the interminable indecision, wrangling, ineptitude, divisiveness and personal ambition of the so-called elite. His powerful rhetoric and presence had given a hope, however tenuous, to a malaise of confusion and mistrust. By securing the Union backing in advance to halt the crippling strikes with promises of the new economic approach, he avoided being labelled with left wing groups like Momentum and appealed directly to the people. His plans, though radical were carefully planned and openly discussed. He was clever in his planning and openness so that any criticism by parliamentary members and the media was identified as 'old school' protectionism.

The Prime Minister's inner three represented an impenetrable trio who, as long as they stood together, could ward off any assaults from within and without.

Archie MacDonald was a dour Scot; he was well schooled in economics and was mean; truly mean; it was said that to enter the gates of the Treasury, you first had to get passed the Scottish Cerberus. It suited McVey to have such a man in charge of the purse strings; before any department came cap in hand to him; they made doubly sure they had clearly detailed all costs and benefits. He knew the added bonus was MacDonald's unswerving loyalty to him; they went back many years to their Union days.

Toby Fennel was made Home Secretary and was, on the other hand, a politician whose ability to manipulate was surpassed only by his singular ambition. Fennel was another Cerberus but his was an attack dog; no subtlety or finesse about him. He saw himself, one day, as the Prime Minister but was astute enough to bide his time and await the right opportunity. Until that time, McVey knew he had him in his pocket; he knew Fennel would wipe his arse for him if he saw it would gain the PM's favour over his arch rival the Chancellor.

It was therefore, a fine balancing act but McVey knew that his position and his success of maintaining an iron grip on his party, was through the three of them standing united. He had purposefully structured his government so that he could hold it together and pull the necessary strings at the right time. Once in power he set about carefully appointing teams to address each area of the 'rebuilding' and with MacDonald as his Chancellor and Fennel as his Home Secretary, he formed the inner group, a sanctum, that he needed to carefully control everything from a small central base.

However, he soon found that whilst changing the fences and shape around the zoo; the animals retained their spots and stripes. Implementing his plan was harder than he envisaged and the people did not respond with the enthusiasm his planning required. Too many saw the generous subsidies meant as an incentive to work, as an incentive to avoid and harsher measures by the Chancellor, no matter how justified, became further disincentives. Time, that goddess who had manipulated so many before, was to prove an unforgiving deity.

MacDonald and Fennel opened the first fissures; their squabbling first became an irritation to McVey but soon he found that he had to take control of them to avoid public splits. At first he revelled in the power he assumed but, as the old saying goes: 'power corrupts and absolute power corrupts absolutely'. Where ever he found dissent, he took tighter control until it seemed to the critical right wing media and the opposition members, that he had created a sort of presidency or as some nicknamed him: a new Caesar and whispers behind hands prayed for the coming of a Brutus to rid them of this man; they were becoming nervous and some outspoken against the centralising of so much power and the autocracy the PM was assuming. And now there was a 'fifth element'; the IDM.

John McVey came back to the present to hear the Chancellor rambling on about time being the crucial factor. 'So, how long are you talking about?' McVey asked.

'John,' the Chancellor began with his first name again, 'We are not talking about hours or days or weeks. It's a sort of holding pattern we need. We are moving into the summer period when trade and work will pick up.'

'And holidays,' Fennel put in.

MacDonald chose to ignore him. 'I can guarantee that by the end of summer, let's say September, we'll see a significant shift in the financial situation.'

'And then we move into the cold, bleak winter,' Fennel almost sang it.

The Chancellor sat upright and glared at him. 'It is that sort of attitude that has caused a lot of our problems.' He turned his head slowly away from the Home Secretary and stared at the Prime Minister; he spoke slowly. 'I know in the past you have drawn certain lines we should not cross over, but each day I see those few who have so much.'

Fennel almost giggled. 'Oh, we're back on that one are we? Let's tax the rich. There's plenty of moolah there. Well, Mister Chancellor, for a start, most of their money is off-shore and it will be Hell's own job to get at it. We'll spend as much on lawyer's fees as we shall recover. Besides the fact, it was in our manifesto that we shall not bankrupt the country, which we would surely do, if we focussed on the rich. They do own 90 percent of industry.'

Fennel sat back, satisfied he had fired off a broadside without a response. The PM left a few moments to elapse before speaking.

'Toby is right. In fact, you are both right but now is not the time. We shall, I promise, one day address this imbalance of wealth but we shall need a very subtle approach. We need to trap the organ grinder's monkey, not shoot it.'

'A nice metaphor, John,' Fennel ventured the PM's first name.

MacDonald ground his teeth. 'You, the pair of you,' he surprisingly included the PM, 'blame me for our economic problems but while you tie my hands, I am like a juggler with too many balls. There, that is another metaphor for you!'

'Alright, enough of this,' the PM interceded. 'What you really mean is that your plan for a spring boost failed. Archie, we can't go on like this. Have you seen the latest polls for the IDM? They're carving into us; there are two more bi-elections coming up which we will be lucky to hold on to and there are threats of more defections. You made a recent suggestion to raise more money by raising certain taxes but you didn't put a precise figure on it. I must have cast iron calculations.'

'Not just another mountain of beans,' Fennel added with a smirk.

The Chancellor's lips moved as he ground his teeth again and looked scathingly at the Home Secretary. 'You know, it would be helpful to everyone if you gave your brain a chance before your arse spoke empty words.' He hurried on before the Home Secretary had chance of reply. 'Do you know what he said last night on Sky News?' He leaned forward so that his face was nearer the Prime Minister's. 'When asked about the leaks of confidential emails to the Press, he said he was reviewing and reclassifying public and private information. He said too much was being made of freedom of speech and the 'free Press' as along with that freedom there had to be responsibility and respect without which the Government would be obliged to step in.'

'I said, "I may have to step in under certain circumstances", you see, you are misquoting me as much as the media. I am fucking sick of these pencil pushers who paint us in the darkest light.'

'And how light can the dark be?' the Chancellor chortled at Fennel's confused metaphor.

'Those latest leaks will cause untold damage; not only to our economy, which you should be concerned about,' Fennel addressed to the Prime Minister, 'but the Foreign Secretary is blowing blood vessels over the reaction from the U.S. and the French. It is time...'

But the Prime Minister cut him off. 'I think it was Steinbeck who wrote something like: "when people read, they paint pictures from the words using the colours according to their predilections". You should remember that Toby.'

The Chancellor smiled but the Home Secretary felt it an admonishment, even though he did not have a clue what the PM was talking about. He had never read Steinbeck and painting pictures with words was for mamby-pamby poets for whom, obviously, he had no time for.

'Now,' the Prime Minister brought his hands together, pressing his fingers like the small steeple of a village chapel, 'let's get to the heart of this problem.'

* * *

So why did the rise of the Independent Democratic Movement; the IDM, cause him so much concern? Why was it more than the brief thorns of the past with the DLP and the 'famous four', and UKIP with Farage? There were many reasons; to begin with its conception arose from the wasted Brexit years and a population wearied by the pandemic and the interminable indecision, wrangling, and divisiveness and personal ambition that was exposed over a prolonged period of time. The 'Party System' became the 'touch paper' and when a spark was applied, it flared quickly into a fireball. The Media, needing a new 'Altar of News', eagerly stoked the flames and from it, an idea became a living entity that many saw as a viable alternative to part and cross the waters of years of inertia.

Then there was the exposure of Executive power. The British populous were bemused by the Trump era; a man who bullied and lied and cajoled and fired those nearest to him if they disagreed with him. A man who made 'executive' decisions without apparent opposition: climate change, racial intolerance, Covid-19 denial; and all this after a dubious election which he deflected for four years and then tried, without evidence to question the validity of Biden's election to replace him.

At the same time, Putin flouted the very heart of democracy with autocratic rulings even to the extent of proposing a change to ensure he could remain President for a lifetime. Russia was caught too many times with its hands in the cookie jar with doping in many sports including exposure during the Olympics and with the use of different, toxic drugs to eliminate so-called dissidents to the State and fake accusations to jail opposition members who became a threat to Putin's position and for all these, internally and internationally, the blame was firmly placed at Putin's feet. Finally, he exposed himself to the western world with his invasion of Ukraine. His almost daily proclamations of 'overcoming a Nazi state' as his excuse would not even convince the most gullible, but the extraordinary failure of his 'Imperial' forces while trying to emulate a Tsar of a strong empire, made people of the west query the very power of individuals in power throughout the west. Putin had not only misjudged the will and resistance of the Ukrainians but his life endeavour to dissemble the West had backfired catastrophically with the strengthening of NATO and alignment of Europe with the US.

This focussed the British people on our own 'Executive' power; those who appeared to make decisions without the proper authority or procedure; some saw Boris Johnson as a mini-Trump and he was not alone to fall under the focus of the public but more important, that of the media.

At first, McVey and his small band of three appeared to working to short cut to implementing needed policies but it quickly became apparent that McVey was autocratic and bullying and his soft, persuasive words to the general public were undermined by his actions. The Independent Democratic Movement highlighted all his failings and proposed a new system where no man held enough power, except in times of national emergencies. They proposed a government made up of independent members; a no party system; who elected a leader and the entire Cabinet with the power to remove any individual who put ambition above duty.

The sudden wind of change, fanned the ideas into a credible alternative and throughout the country, small groups began to meld together to form in towns and cities, and then regional organisations. Inadvertently, Kier Starmer had encouraged the ripple to become a wave by announcing that he wanted to devolve more power to the regions. This, coupled with the growing distrust of the growing centralisation of power, fanned the ideas and aspirations of those who sought more independence from Westminster and the autocratic power of McVey.

Then there came a swelling of the younger element; the youth at schools and universities; but not just student elements but also the young workers. At first, the older politically sensible generation dismissed it as the usual left wing aggressors; a resurgence of Momentum but it quickly became clear that these younger elements were the same as those who rallied behind climate change and other world initiatives. It became more than a populist idea; it became a movement. Several MP's gave their support and the new Movement was formed with an identity. The first shock waves came from two bi-elections; one a safe Tory stronghold and the other a safe Labour seat. Majorities of over twenty thousand and twelve thousand, respectively, were overturned and the first IDM members were elected.

Seven disconsolate MP's from the main parties; defected to the IDM and when challenged to put up their seats for re-election, they did so and were returned with larger majorities. At the following local elections, IDM candidates swept in and took over eleven councils and returned over three hundred councillors.

The IDM had become, in a matter of just over two years, a credible alternative. Why had this been allowed to happen by the main parties; because of the inertia and personal ambition they had been accused of; they had expected that something so radical would slowly wilt on the vine as impulsive enthusiasm usually does; but their main misjudgement was that it was not an impulse but a deep heart felt desire for a change by the people.

* * *

Marcus had left Downing Street by the rear entrance to avoid the Press and cameras which were ever present at the front. He returned to his office and worked through his lunch break and the afternoon on his 'special project'. He tried to blank the episode with his father from his mind but when he paused, it intruded and he sat for long periods building the hate he had but at the same time, questioning the quest he was embarking on. It was passed five-o-clock when the phone rang on his desk. He left his drawing board and went to his desk and lifted the receiver.

'Marcus, it is Helen here. TJ would like to see you before you leave,'

Marcus said he would be right up and busied himself putting his drawings away by rolling them into cardboard tubes and then locking them away in a metal cabinet; the firm was very strict on the security of their projects. He took the lift to the top floor and entered Helen's office.

'Working late?' he asked.

Helen simply smiled, 'Go right in, Marcus, he's waiting for you.'

TJ's office while being large, did not reflect the Chairman's position; the room was almost bland with just a large desk, a few chairs around a small table to one side and several cabinets. The walls were undecorated with pictures or plaques and the carpet had seen better days. It all reflected a man who was business like in his approach and scorned the trappings of showing off wealth and success. TJ himself was in his sixties; he was tall and slim with a full head of grey hair; he was neatly dressed but not in Saville Row and he gave the appearance of restrained eloquence.

'Ah Marcus,' he said quietly, 'come and sit down. Get one of those chairs.'

Marcus retrieved a chair from the small table area and placed it in front of TJ's desk. 'So tell me, how is your project for Lakeland going?'

Marcus had expected this to be the subject TJ had called him for to discuss so he had prepared himself.

'I had a meeting with him and his wife last Thursday and took them both to the site.'

Lakeland was a very old friend of TJ's from the States and had told him he wanted to build a new home for him and his new wife – his third actually. She had not travelled much outside the States and he wanted to impress her with a country style mansion in the 'pastures of England' but of course, not that far from London where he had set up his own European headquarters.

Over an extended lunch when Lakeland had demonstrated how much of the 'English fare' he could consume and TJ had restricted himself to a simple fish dish; he had outlined what he imagined he desired. He wanted not an existing old style mansion but a new site with a house designed to reflect the old style but was in fact, inside, filled with 'modern'.

TJ had assigned the 'special' project to Marcus, outlining the needs but also warning him that Lakeland having virtually unlimited resources, would demand anything and everything and the real test for Marcus would be to find a site and then design a structure that finely balanced the old and modern but to expect changes according to Lakeland's whim or his expectation of what 'old style' looked like.

'So how did that go?' TJ enquired.

'It went very well; his wife was particularly impressed with the site and the area. Lakeland said he would have a copse of trees removed and I had a hard time explaining that they were mature beech trees and would add to the ambience of the area. It would also probably hinder his planning application if he removed the trees.'

'I expect you had to explain the meaning of ambience.' TJ smiled.

'Actually, his wife is quite an educated woman, degrees from Harvard, so Lakeland impressed upon me, and she took over and explained to him that the beech genre were among the most elegant of trees with their grey bark and would encourage wild life like squirrels.'

TJ began to chuckle. 'I wish I could have been there.'

'His wife, Arlene, has been a great help. She has a clear perspective of what she wants for the house and the surrounds. I think that as the project progresses, she will come to the fore and Lakeland will take a back seat and that will make my task far easier. He had seen an example of an atrium when they were in Rome at some ancient Roman site, and he wondered if I could include an atrium.'

TJ chuckled some more. 'And what did you say to that?'

'I didn't have to say anything. His wife interjected and told him not to be stupid as it would not fit in with her ideas.'

'Good, good,' TJ said, 'have you an estimated target in mind?'

'I think the spring or summer next year is achievable depending upon him finalising the design and the planning application being approved in good time.'

TJ ran a finger along his mouth and paused. 'Actually, there is another more pressing matter I wanted to talk to you about.'

He lifted an early edition of the evening newspaper and turned it round to face Marcus so that he could read the front page headline. Marcus's heart sank but before he could speak, TJ continued. 'When you first mentioned to me that you were becoming involved with the IDM, I was quite specific when I said that what you did in your own time was your personal affair but this is making it public.'

Marcus read the headline: 'PM's Son to Speak at IDM Conference'.

'I did not expect it to be made public until I gave the go ahead. I saw my father this morning; I did not expect him to release it to the Press.'

'I doubt very much that it was your father's doing; had you told anyone at the Movement that you wanted to keep it under wraps for a while?' TJ's voice remained calm but Marcus could sense an underlying admonishment.

'I am sorry TJ; it is not what I wanted. I felt

that I should tell my father but I never saw this consequence.'

'Never the less, it has a consequence and I do not want my firm involved. Helen has already had to fend off enquiries from the media. I certainly do not want hordes of pressmen and television cameras surrounding my offices. I think it better if you work from home or find some place away that you can work without their interruption. For now, Lakeland's special project is your one and only priority.'

Marcus stood, shaken by what was suddenly happening. 'You are not sacking me?' he asked.

TJ shook his head and smiled. 'When I took you on, I saw in you an architect with great potential and vision. I still believe that. You have made a mistake; a stupid mistake; but I think we can ride this out. Now, get together what you need, secrete yourself away somewhere and concentrate on this special Lakeland project. Quite frankly, I think it better that you do not come into the office for a while. At least until this Conference has been held. Hopefully things will die down after that.' TJ paused and stared at Marcus waiting for a response but when one was not forthcoming, he added, 'I would seriously think about your commitment to this Movement. I don't know what you hope to achieve by making a speech for them but think about what it may do to your career.'

'TJ I am most sorry and I am grateful you are still

giving me a chance. I.... I shall work on with this project and not let what is happening with the IDM affect it. I'll tell Helen where I am working from.'

TJ nodded and Marcus turned and left his office. Helen gave him a weak smile as he departed; why was it secretaries always knew about everything that was going on?

Marcus entered his apartment and heard Katie cooking something in the kitchen. He hung up his coat and glanced round the corner of the doorway and watched her for a minute as she busied herself arranging saucepans on the cooker and adjusting the heat under them.

He admired everything about her; her blonde hair always tied back in a long pony tail except when she went to bed with him and then he marvelled how it cascaded around her face, accentuating her high cheeks bones and the darkest of brown, feline eyes which always mesmerised him. Her body was slim and muscular due to her working as an instructor at a gymnasium and her buttocks were tight in her hugging leggings and were always the cause of a certain stirring in his loins.

She sensed she was being watched and turned her head. Her smile was tight lipped and said; 'I should be pleased to see you but I'm not sure I am'. She replaced a lid on a saucepan, adjusted the heat and faced him. 'So, did you see your father?'

Marcus stepped into the room, he wanted to kiss her, he wanted to say many things but a lot had lately passed between them and Katie was standing her ground and to his mind, a little obstinately. He put his mobile phone on the table and reached out for her but she stepped away and busied herself getting cutlery from a drawer.

'Yes, I did see him but it went as I expected.' He sighed and shrugged to himself. 'But I shall still go ahead with the speech.'

She faced him with knives and forks clutched in her hands. 'What about your job? What about our wedding plans? What about the effect your speech will have on all that? I imagine you will be hounded by the press; I don't want that in my life.'

He thought he should tell her about his meeting with TJ but that would only serve to harden her resolve so he went instead to his work room. To one side was his draughtsman's easel with a high stool and on a side table all his working tools; laptop, pencils, stencils, slides and drawing instruments. He laid his bag carrying his folder of copious notes for the project on a table and then went over to a cabinet, unlocked it and stored the tubes with his drawings for the 'special project'. He had not decided yet if he would work from here or relocate but that would mean moving all his equipment. Like everything at that moment, he deferred making a decision.

He re-entered the kitchen and Katie was looking at his mobile phone.

'Why are you looking at my phone?'

She held it up in front of him so he could see the text on the screen. 'It's from your girlfriend, Diana. She asks if you are still going to see her tonight.'

Marcus stood, frozen, he had forgotten all about his promise to see her; it was just another error he had made; it seemed they were unending this day.

Katie half put, half dropped the phone onto the table and she pushed passed him. Marcus stood still without moving until he heard her in the hall, putting on her coat. He went out to her but she spoke first. 'I'm going back into my apartment. I think we both need some time alone to think things through.'

'Please Katie, don't go. We need to talk about this, not just think about it. I need to explain a lot to you, I know, but it is not what you think. Please!'

Katie looked at him with a face that clearly showed her anger. 'I think you are making a lot of mistakes and the biggest one is that Diana. Get yourself sorted out and then, maybe, we can talk about it.'

She went in to the kitchen and slipped off the ring from her finger and then turned and quickly walked passed him and opened the door, she left and closed it behind her without another word.

Marcus just stood for a moment in the hall but then a hiss from the kitchen reminded him that Katie had left the dinner cooking and a saucepan must be boiling over. He went to the cooker and turned off the power to the hob and then to the oven; he had lost all appetite for a meal that evening. He wandered aimlessly around the kitchen for a moment and then noticed that she had left her engagement ring by his mobile phone. He picked it up and turned it between his fingers and then put it down again.

He went into the lounge and slumped onto the sofa. His thoughts of the many troubles began to crowd in on him: his father, his job, TJ, Katie, the speech and of course, Diana. It was then that his phone began to ring and he went back to the kitchen and picked up his mobile. For a moment he thought it may be Katie having second thoughts but the name and screen picture showed it was Diana. He pressed the answer button.

'Darling,' she said; her voice as soft and enchanting as always. 'I sent a text but you did not respond. I do hope we are still on for tonight.' Then she added, 'At my place at eight.'

Marcus crumpled inside. 'Yes, of course. I'll be there.' He ended the call and then cursed himself; he should be saying no and then making his way to Katie's apartment to bare his soul to her; so why did he say yes? But he knew inside why and at eight-o-clock he would be proving why.

* * *

It had been nearly three months before when he had read an article in a Sunday newspaper about the Independent Democratic Movement. It was written by a reporter who was clearly supportive of their aims and went into some detail about its objectives and benefits over the existing, archaic party system. It gave notice of a support and recruitment evening at a London hotel and Marcus, inquisitively, had attended.

The evening had started with speeches, purposefully kept brief, by the chairman Sir Rees Lipton and the Treasurer and Secretary John Wilder who succinctly expressed the aims and policies of the Movement. Leaflets were distributed giving the overall aims and strategy of the Movement and this was followed by light refreshments and a chance to mingle with members and ask questions.

John Wilder noted Marcus's presence and knowing who he was, had a quiet word with his chairman who agreed Marcus should be given special attention. Wilder moved across the room to Diana Bright, the Head of Administration, and pointed out Marcus standing to one side and alone; reading a leaflet. He suggested that she might be the right person to attract Marcus into the Movement.

Diana looked across and admired the handsome young man; so this was the Prime Minister's son; she nodded to Wilder and made her way over to Marcus.

'Have you liked what you have heard so far?' Diana asked Marcus as she moved to his side; her voice was soft, almost like water slipping over stones.

Marcus looked up from the leaflet he had been reading. For a moment he found words difficult to assemble into a coherent response. Diana was a flame redhead whose hair cascaded over her shoulders but the part of her that caught Marcus momentarily spell bound was her emerald eyes which seemed to sparkle amid the beauty of her face. Her eye lashes were long and she displayed these to advantage by slowly fluttering them as she spoke. Her mouth was wide and full and her lips blood red and when she smiled, she revealed perfect white teeth, and she seemed to be smiling permanently.

Marcus managed to gather himself enough to respond, 'Interesting. Yes, definitely interesting; especially Sir Rees Lipton's talk on Need and Want. And you are?'

Diana introduced herself and then said, 'And you are Marcus McVey.'

Marcus blushed slightly. 'Will you hold that against me?'

Diana laughed; a soft sound issuing from her lips which teased him with expectation. 'I would not hold anything against you.' Her lips smiled with a hidden meaning. 'Unless of course; you would like me to.'

Marcus became aware he had a growing sensation emanating from his loins.

'I am just joking,' she said, 'perhaps you would like to come with me to a side room we have prepared for special guests where we can talk about the Movement in more detail. There's coffee there too. Would you like one?' she asked and moved away before he had a chance to answer and he followed her into the room.

Diana poured him a cup of coffee not adding milk or sugar without asking; she had sized him up. She spoke with a quiet, almost melodious voice but with an intense conviction. They had sat with her chair close to him so that he was aware of her presence and her perfume and she maintained eye contact that prevented him from being distracted and looking away.

She briefly outlined the aims again but in a succinct way and supporting each point with comments how it was the new way to replace the old archaic party system.

'You know, right back to the origins of the Whigs and Tories, there has always been that underlying bond of party loyalty that prohibited not only individual voices but was the will of the few in power, not the majority who put them there.'

At the end, she told him she thought he could be a valuable member to have in the Movement.

'Because of who I am,' he said, not impressed.

'Quite frankly, yes,' she freely admitted. 'If you joined us and truly believed in our ideals, then I can see you can be a great benefit.' And then she added in very soft tone; 'And you will be to me especially. I am responsible for coordinating and organising the Movement. I see that things like the forthcoming conference go well; subjects are assessed and prioritised, speakers are selected; you know; all that sort of thing.'

'Sounds very important but do you not have a team to assist?'

She sighed, 'I do but we are still in our infancy, compared with the existing parties. I think I need someone younger like you to assist me as a sort of personal adviser.'

'Do you think I am qualified for that?' he queried.

She smiled and leaned closer. 'I have an instinct you would. I am a good judge of people and I think you and I could make a good team. It's unpaid, unfortunately, so why don't you take a bit of time to think it over.' She passed him a card. 'That's my phone and my address.'

Sometimes one makes a hasty decision and is not sure why except it feels right as an opportunity. A few days later he met her again and he told her that in whatever capacity she wanted him he was willing to at least give it a try. She put her hand on his arm and squeezed it gently; 'I will need you, Marcus. I believe you and I could make a great team together. Can you commit your time and yourself to me?'

Marcus committed himself. Over the following weeks, they attended meetings together and eventually, perhaps by design, they met one evening in her apartment to go over the structure the Movement needed to consolidate its position with the public. As it became aware to Marcus, she had prepared the document and really wanted only for him to show his approval. By this time, he was almost completely besotted with her and it was enough just to be in her company.

As they sat on the sofa, Diana smiled and leaned into him, 'Thank you, Marcus, I appreciate the time you are giving. I know you are a busy lad with your firm.'

He was not happy by the way she had called him 'lad'. 'How old do you think I am?'

Diana eased back from him. 'That is a strange question?'

'You called me 'lad'; that makes me think you see me only as a young boy?'

She moved closer again and placed a hand on his shoulder. 'Oh no, it was just an expression. You are young compared with most of the old cronies in the Movement,' she laughed, 'I find you refreshing but not a boy.' She put her face close to his, 'Could you show me what sort of man you are?'

Their eyes locked and then Marcus felt his mouth drawn to hers and they kissed. Again, there are times when things apparently move so quickly that you are not aware what followed and shall not remember exactly how they happened; but what Marcus would always remember was the feel of her warm flesh, her soft body and engulfing legs as she wound herself around him, her lips driving him down as she turned him on his back and literally speared herself on him. His eyes became unseeing but his brain, through a haze of searing sensations, felt she was consuming him.

When he awoke, he found he was in her bed but wasn't quite sure how they had arrived there; he had blurred memories of motion and clothing being discarded and then something akin to a dream. She leaned over him, her breasts prominent to his face and she smiled as she offered him a glass of white wine.

She rolled away and retrieved her own glass from a side table and sipped it. He sipped his own wine, it was chilled and he felt it slip refreshingly down his throat. They were both lying on the bed, both naked and he let his eyes pass down her incredible body. Physically he felt exhausted but mentally he felt exhilarated and a fanfare of trumpets would not have been amiss.

That is how it had all started and whilst his

conscience was an ever companion reminding him of his infidelity; he could not break free from the emerald promise of her eyes, even as Kate's suspicions grew.

The next time they met at her apartment, she had already prepared a cool glass of white wine for him and guided him over to the sofa. He noticed she sat slightly apart from him.

'Is there something wrong?' he asked. 'You seem a little tense.'

She dipped a finger in her drink and swirled it around before sucking on her finger tip. 'You mentioned once that you and your father are not close.' He made to respond but she continued. 'In fact, one time you told me just how far apart you are. You mentioned your mother and how your father treated her and you.'

Marcus remembered the conversation; it was just after making love when they lay side by side and she had stroked his face. He had mentioned his mother used to do that when he was very young and upset from another bruising encounter with his father.

'It was not a happy childhood, I admit, he was too engrossed in his career and his ambition to see how neglected he left mother and me.'

She moved a little closer on the sofa. 'And how do you feel towards him now?'

He shrugged. 'The same; he hasn't changed. In

fact now he is Prime Minister he has no time for me at all but that suits me. I have my own life now.'

Diana reached across and touched his arm and then slowly slid her hand down until she grasped his hand. 'You do realise that for us to make gains with the public, we shall have to attack the Labour party and specifically, we shall have to target him.'

Marcus blew a laugh through his lips. 'He's a big enough target.'

'But how would you feel about it?'

Marcus needed to give that little thought and after only a brief pause he said, 'I would wholly support it. I do not feel I owe him anything. Why do you ask? Have you developed some strategy against him?'

Diana hesitated. 'I was speaking with Rees about the conference we shall be having. He said, as an aside really, that we need a speaker who would really make an impact. I'm sorry, darling,' her face moved even closer to his, 'I said wouldn't it be special if you made a speech.'

Marcus moved away from her, more in surprise; 'Me? Make a speech?'

'I think you would make a good one and just think, if you aimed at the party system, it would resonate with the media and the public.'

'Just because I am the Prime Minister's son?' he queried.

Diana simply said, 'Think about it. Have a word

with Rees as well; he thought it would be a good idea.' She got up and went into the bedroom.

Marcus did think about it for a long while until Diana returned. She had undressed and slipped on a white bath robe that was pulled tight and showed every curve. 'I'm going to have a shower, do you mind?'

He was a bit disappointed as it seemed like a dismissal but he shook his head. 'Perhaps I had better get home; you have given me a lot to think about.' He stood up.

It was Diana's turn to look disappointed and she moved close to him until her hip brushed against his side and her hand touched his arm. 'Oh, I was hoping you might soap my back.' She smiled to reveal all her teeth.

'Soap your back in a shower? It would mean I have to shower with you.'

'Unless you want to stand outside and reach in.' Diana smiled in a young girlish way. 'Do you object?'

'Is this a softening up technique?'

She kissed him lightly on the lips. 'Who said anything about being soft?'

* * *

At eight-o-clock he found himself ringing the doorbell to her apartment which was opened almost immediately. She smiled, 'Always prompt. Come in, we have things to discuss.'

As he followed her in he felt disappointed; no kiss; no hug; 'So what was so important that you had to see me?'

Diana looked back at him, noting his petulant tone. 'I wanted to talk to you about your speech; of course.'

'You know I have agreed to make it?'

'Of course I do. Rees called me and told me you had agreed to speak at the conference.' She saw that his expression had not changed and she stepped closer to him and linked her arm around his waist. She frowned, 'What are you angry about?'

'I specifically told the Chairman when we discussed my making the speech, that I wanted it to be kept a secret for a while and, I would write it myself with no editing.' He stepped back to unlink her arm. 'Now it seems everyone knows about it. It has even appeared in the evening papers and God knows where else, the television news probably. And now you want to discuss it! Perhaps you are going to suggest you write it for me.'

Diana stood with a sad and hurt look on her face. 'Sweetheart, I was not going to do such a thing. Of course I knew you had spoken with Rees about it. I was just going to offer my help. If you wanted it, that is.'

The word 'sweetheart' took him by surprise; it was the first time she had used it. 'But I told Rees I wanted to write it myself. Then what do you want?' he asked, slightly more quietly.

Her lips parted to reveal her pink tongue and she reached forward and slowly slid her arms round his waist. 'I just wanted to talk about it. I want to help you as you have been helping me.' She made an exaggerated sigh; 'Rees told me not to tell anyone. I don't know who has leaked it to the Press, Rees certainly would not; he is too much of a gentleman.' She moved her body closer until they were touching. 'Please do not be angry with me.' Then she giggled, 'Come into the bedroom with me. Perhaps we can discuss things better in there.'

Something clicked in his head; her suggestion was too obvious and he knew she was trying to seduce him only to discuss his speech. He stepped away from her again and avoided looking into those mesmeric green eyes. 'No, I'm sorry but I must be going.'

'What?'

He moved towards the door. 'I'll give you a call,' and then added; 'When I have written the speech.' He looked back as he opened the door. 'We can go through it then.'

Diana said nothing; she was too surprised that probably for the first time in her life; someone had walked out on her.

On the drive back to his apartment he regretted leaving Diana like that but for some reason, he felt better for doing it; a small barb had been released from his heart. When he returned to his apartment, he rang his Uncle Robert; his father's brother; and asked if he could go and stay with him and his two daughters for a few days. He made the excuse that work had been getting him down and his relationship with a girl was not going well. Robert McVey had said no excuses were needed and he was welcome to stay as long as he liked.

CHAPTER TWO
DARKER, DARKER GROWS THE HOUR

Matheson pulled his car to the side of the road, switched off the lights and engine and settled back in his seat to wait. It was raining steadily which suited him; it meant few people would be about and the rain would make the windows opaque.

It had been six months earlier that he had been summoned to the office of his Head of the Department, Edward Staniforth. He had stood outside the large double doors and surrendered his mobile phone and was scanned for any electronic devices. The Head always ensured that visitors to his room had no listening devices on their person. He stepped in and the door was closed behind him.

Staniforth was seated at a very large, ornate desk, and was writing with a fountain pen; one of the few men that Matheson knew who preferred the nib and ink to an electronic terminal which he used only for certain internal memorandum. Matheson guessed rightly that the Head did this as a pen could not be compromised. He looked up briefly and waved Matheson to a chair in front of the desk and did not look up again until he had finished writing and had screwed the top to the pen which he now, as he sat back, twirled between his fingers.

'John, I have a special task for you,' his voice was crisp and as usual, what he had to say would be short and precise; words and time were rarely wasted. 'I want you to set up a special unit, say four or five should do, to infiltrate and monitor the IDM.'

'And this is for?' Matheson enquired.

'This is a request from the PM. He is concerned that they may have been infiltrated by others who, shall we say, do not quite share their ideals. I must say they do seem a pretty rum bunch but the PM's concerned that they do seem to be having some success.' He coughed to allow himself a pause. 'Mind you, I reckon the PM is just getting a little nervous at their success with local elections and some defections. I doubt if there is anything really wrong but we ought to keep an eye on them.'

'Is this strictly legal?' Matheson asked.

'No but only if you do something which is not legal.' Staniforth tilted his head to one side as if making a statement and forming a question at the same time.

'And this request from the Prime Minister; is this just from him or is it a Government request?'

Staniforth shuffled in his chair. 'For the moment, let's just assume it is from the PM. I think...' he paused and chose his words. 'He is in a spot of bother and is casting his net to see what kind of fish he may catch.'

Matheson smiled inwardly; that was closer to the mark, he guessed. 'Who do I report to?'

Staniforth had heavy brows and a large beak nose and when he smiled, he looked more like the hawk that had earned him that nickname. He now smiled, 'Gilroy will look after your budget and you shall report solely to the PM.'

So you can keep your arse clean, Matheson thought, while the PM will be hung out to dry if anything went wrong like this becoming public knowledge.

'I assume there will be no written orders,' Matheson said, knowing the answer.

'Good Lord no; it is after all, the PM's idea,' Staniforth answered immediately. 'It will also help to keep you on your toes.' He smiled again. 'And keep the PM on his. He's not going to use this department as a political football; you should know the rules by now. I'll leave you to pick your own team and see Gilroy about a budget. It will be tight but generous.'

Matheson wondered how he would square 'tight but generous'. 'If anything goes....' Matheson hesitated. 'If anything should go untoward..... I mean, if I should consider that we are being compromised by the PM?' He left the rest of the question hanging.

Staniforth said nothing for a moment but stared at him from under his heavy brows. 'Use your initiative;

that is why I have selected you for this task.'

He saw that Matheson just looked back at him with an expression that bordered on insubordination but as that was a quality he admired in Matheson; step close to the border but not across; he said, 'If it gets really marginal and we, as a department could be compromised, and only then, you can contact me. I shall contact you from time to time. Just for an update, you realise.'

'I assume MI5 and MI6 or any other of the security services will not be in the circle.'

Staniforth said nothing but very slowly moved his head from side to side.

Matheson had to be satisfied with that and however he felt, over the following weeks, he assembled a team of three specially chosen for their varied skills; planned out a strategy and put them to work reporting only to him. He had a secret meeting with the PM who was more concerned with the secrecy of the operation than the ethics of what he was asking for; Matheson gave him a mobile phone with only a special number on it and appraised the PM of using it to the minimum. They had met once before at this same location and it was a call from the PM that afternoon that brought him here now.

* * *

He saw the lights of a car pull in behind his and the lights switched off. Matheson reached forward under the steering column and flicked a switch; he had activated a recording device; he was equally determined not to be hung out to dry. A heavy figure in a trilby pulled low over his face and wearing a dark overcoat, exited the rear door of the car and walk slowly towards his car. The door opened and the PM dropped heavily in the passenger seat and closed the door.

The PM sat for a moment, his breath suggested he was somewhat stressed at the risk of the meeting. 'Have you anything to report?' he asked without offering any form of greeting.

'As you know, I have all my men in place. At the moment they are looking into the structure and all the top personnel involved and activities; direct and personal. Apart from the usual small drug taking and shall we say, personal relationships, we have yet to discover any political activities of a suspicious nature.' The PM sighed heavily with irritation. 'We are looking into some of the sponsors. One in particular may bear fruit.'

The PM looked across at him. 'What sort of fruit?'

'A rotten apple,' Matheson replied. 'Just a lead at the moment but we are following it through.'

The PM looked forward and was quiet for a while. 'I suppose you heard the news today?'

'About your son; yes, it was in most evening papers. An embarrassment I assume.'

'More than that,' the PM said with vehemence. 'I want you to look into him.'

It was Matheson's turn to look across at the PM. 'Your son, to look for what?'

'Anything at all; it is obvious they are using him. I thought he had more sense; I spent enough on his education.' The PM reached for the door handle. 'I want no preferential treatment for him either. Keep digging,' he paused, 'but dig deeper. Let me know what you find.' He opened the door and hefted his large frame out of the car.

Matheson waited until the other car had driven away before he switched off the recording device and started his engine and drove across to the south side of London; there was one special man he had to see.

Matheson stepped up to the door of a nondescript terraced house and rang the doorbell; he saw the bell light up and guessed rightly that it was now scanning him and passing a picture to a mobile phone in the house. 'It's me, Sam.' A moment later the door opened and Sam White stood there; he was in his sixties, a small man with thinning white hair and dressed in sagging trousers and a loose woollen cardigan over his shirt.

'Come in', he said and stood back to allow Matheson to enter through the narrow doorway.

'I hope I am not disturbing you, Sam. I know it is rather late. I was worried you may have retired to your bed.'

Sam closed the door. 'No, I was just putting the finishing touches to this signal box,' he held up a small model of a railway signal box in his left hand.

Matheson looked at it keenly. 'That is quite exquisite. I assume you have a railway layout. I didn't know you went in for modelling.'

Sam chuckled, 'There is a lot you do not know about me.'

Matheson smiled, he was always amused at the way Sam laughed, a cross between a Disney chip monk and mewing cat. 'That's true. Can you show me the layout?'

Sam led the way to the back room and Matheson followed him in and then stopped with amazement. What he had called a layout was in fact a whole village and railway which spanned the entire room.

The track wound its way from a station at the front, round the far end and climbed a slight incline up onto a seven arch viaduct across the back and then back round to the station. The station at the front had two platforms and a green Southern train was halted at one platform with people about to get on and a woman leading a porter pushing a trolley with a her luggage while others sat on benches. Two people were crossing over the lines on a trellis bridge and the gates to the level crossing were closed and cars and a bus, all to scale, were waiting for the train to leave and the gates to open. In the centre was a small village green with a cluster of trees with green plastic foliage. Some children were playing with a dog while their parents sat and watched from a wooden bench. On the far side there was a square towered church with the vicar poised at the door. Around one side of the green was a parade of shops where people were walking and looking in the windows. Cars were parked by the kerb and a London Transport bus was just turning the corner to arrive at a bus stop where several people waited. To the right, Sam had built a small goods yard where several trucks were linked together to a small shunting engine; one truck was positioned against the opening of a delivery bay and men were hauling large crates from the boxcar wagon. On a small rise, Sam had positioned another church; this one a grey stone church with a grave yard to one side with ornamental graves; angels included. To the side of the church, there were several dwellings; some cottages and a larger detached house.

'Sam!' Matheson exclaimed, 'this is so much more than just a railway model. What period is this?'

'It's around the forties and fifties, nothing precise.' Sam beamed, 'It's my alternate world, actually.' Matheson looked bemused so Sam went on to explain. 'Outside this room, the world has billions of people who are living and dying, sleeping and working, loving and fighting. But inside here, there is this village; my village, my world. This is my haven from all that happens elsewhere. The trick is to keep the two worlds apart.'

Matheson nodded. 'I can understand that. I sometimes wish I could get away from reality, just for a short while. Can you set a train moving for me?'

Sam chuckled again, 'Here, you'll like this. This is the Duchess of Abicorn, an LNER mail train.' He hooked a small plastic mail bag to a hook on a mast near the station and then set a switch on the control panel. From a siding, a maroon liveried steam engine with three carriages moved onto the main track and rounded the bend to the station. As the last carriage passed the mast, a small door swung open and collected the mail bag. The train passed through and rounded the far bend and began climbing the incline up the viaduct. As it levelled out, the train entered a tunnel before appearing further on.

Matheson was enchanted. 'That was incredible. Did you build this all yourself?' he enquired.

'Of course; it's my secret therapy to happiness and calm. It has taken me a few years and I'm still not finished. I get as much satisfaction from the planning and building as I do running the trains. I want to expand the village to include some cottages around this side of the green and some fields with sheep or cows...'

Matheson cut him off, remembering why he had called. 'Another time, Sam, I have come to talk.' He paused, 'And to ask for some personal advice.'

Sam halted the train and switched off the system. He looked at Matheson carefully. In all the years Sam had worked for him, Matheson had never asked for advice, not personal advice, anyway.

Sam led the way into the small front room; it could hardly be called a lounge, it had only room for two armchairs, a sideboard and a small table between the chairs. In the corner was an old fashioned standard lamp. On the sideboard were several books, stacked up neatly and next to them, a small DAB radio. Matheson guessed rightly that there would not be a television in the house.

'Would you like a sherry?' Sam asked and without waiting for a reply, he opened a door to the side board and took out two glasses and a bottle of sherry.

While he did this, Matheson reminisced about the years he had known Sam. He had worked for the Service for, what, must be over nearly forty years. He was never a field operative but had earned himself the highest respect from all the staff and the nickname of 'the librarian' because he had an incredible photographic memory and if you wanted to know something, he knew of it or where it could be found.

He was also talented in the use of computers and had written many routines and algorithms used to decipher or predict.

He had retired a few years back but Matheson had persuaded him to help out on this special project. And so, Sam had managed to get employment with the IDM as an administrator with impeccable references; all false; and had earned the respect of the Movement with his talents and simply from his likeable demeanour.

'What is it I can do?' Sam asked.

Matheson sipped the sherry; it was not remarkable but passable. 'I saw the PM this evening. He's getting itchy feet especially after seeing his son.'

'Ah yes,' Sam said, 'I heard about it on the radio six-o-clock news. I can imagine that has caused him some pain.'

'No, I think their relationship has not been good for some while. I got Roberts to look into it when we first started out. I knew his son had attended a couple of IDM meetings and knew it could complicate matters.'

'And now the PM is getting anxious.'

Matheson put his glass on the table and pressed his fingers together. 'I would say the word should be 'paranoid'. If we do find anything, I think he wants his son implicated.'

Sam stopped sipping his sherry and put the glass

down. 'But that is abominable; what did you say?'

'I said nothing, not to him anyway. I was as shocked as you are. What I need from you, Sam; is to befriend the son, Marcus, and see that he comes to no harm. Make sure there is no one in the Movement that is using him.'

'I have exchanged a few words with him; he seems a decent sort. Alright, I'll see what I can do.'

'It is important that you do, I think by persuading him to make this speech is possibly just a first step. I think they see him as the PM's Achilles heel and want to use him further.'

'I think you may be right; I have noticed that their Head of Administration, a woman called Diana, has been getting close to him. She's a real beauty and I think he may be seeing her outside of hours, so to speak.'

'Alright, I'll get Roberts to make a special check on her. Have you found anything more on Dolan?' Matheson asked, 'He is the one I think we should focus on.'

'Yes, quite a bit; as I told you before, his real name is Dolanski. He's of Polish origin but spent his youthful years in Russia. I have a suspicion, but only a suspicion that he may well have worked for their secret service at one time but I have not confirmed it. He came to this country several years ago and then disappeared. I have now found out he showed up a while later in South America. Mainly in Argentina and he also makes trips to Brazil. I think some of his businesses are worth looking at more closely.'

Sam sipped his sherry before continuing, 'I'm trying to narrow it down and find information on his activities and monies. He has no record of wrong doing but the simple fact there appears to be a curtain around his dealings makes me think there is a lot more to him. He has a sizeable fortune but I'm not sure yet how he made it. I'm pretty sure he may be channelling funds into the IDM through back routes. I have had a bit of good fortune. I worked late one night; a couple of months ago; I used it to ferret around some files, but as I was about to leave I saw James Wilder, the Movement's Treasurer, talking in a room with someone. I'm pretty sure it may have been Dolan.'

'Now that is interesting. It can confirm a link and raises the question, why would Dolan be interested in the IDM?'

Sam chuckled, 'As always, leave it with me. I'll get our little group to ask a special favour from the Met and get them to do some CCTV checks around that date. Maybe we can locate where Dolan has been going and more important, where he is now.'

Matheson plucked his lips with his finger. 'I know you probably think the ethics for this operation are all wrong, Sam, I do not feel comfortable myself. Do you think I was wrong accepting it?'

Sam thought for a moment and then shook his head. 'I realise the position they have put you in but if it was not you then they would have appointed someone else. Your obvious concern for the boy, Marcus, tells me you will tread the line finely. This was always going to be a delicate operation but now Marcus, complicates matters.'

Matheson got to his feet. 'Okay Sam, thank you. You're assurance means a lot. I'll leave you with it but I have a bad feeling in my water that the PM could be our worst enemy in all of this.'

Sam rose and said, 'I agree. I shall move as quickly as I can.' He then chuckled, 'Your water is usually a reliable barometer.'

Matheson allowed a thin smile and then left.

After Matheson had left, Sam took the two glasses into the kitchen and washed them and turned them on their end to drain. All the while, his mind worked away on what Matheson had revealed. It was not with the Prime Minister he thought about; as far as Sam was concerned, he was just a manipulator who felt his grasp slipping when his own son became involved.

No, it was Dolan and Diana. He was sure there was more to be found out about Dolan; possibly drug running or more and he was pretty sure it had been Dolan he had seen with Wilder. The fact that

Wilder held the purse strings of the Movement gave an opportunity for the right, or should he say, the wrong man, to manipulate certain accounts. As for Diana, he had noticed that she had been paying far more attention to Marcus and Sam had noticed on occasion she had secretly touched his hand when talking to him. Now why was she homing in on the young man? He had already agreed to make a speech so why was she still pursuing him? Possibly she really liked him.

Sam had followed them one night, just upon an instinct, and after a meal at a local restaurant near her apartment, they had gone inside her place and at two in the morning, it was obvious Marcus was staying there for the night and a tired but worried Sam, left to go home. He decided it was time for him to get closer to Marcus, not to question his love life but to perhaps, glean a little what she was saying to him.

Sam went into his back room and set the Duchess and the Southern engine in motion. It was at times like this, that he retreated from the real world and allowed his brain to meander through possibilities. It was surprising how many times he had unravelled the twists and turns that clouded his thoughts, just like his engines, that followed the tracks but always ended up back at the station.

He raised his head; now that was a possibility. He felt tired and decided to close down the circuit and head for his own station; in bed.

CHAPTER THREE
STRONG MINDS AND FICKLE HEARTS

Robert McVey's house was situated in the village of Mateley Hill in Gloucestershire. It was Saturday morning and he stood on the front porch taking in the morning air and he felt a chill in the air despite the clear sky and it was supposed to be the third week of spring. He did notice the grass was beginning to grow and regretted the coming season of frequent mowing; pushing and pulling the ancient mower which resisted his attempts to create stripes. The borders too, with so many plants that he knew not their names, would require constant attention.

His wife had known them all and had spent so many hours on her knees weeding and nursing each plant. He missed her so much, especially the way her back would arch and accentuate the roundness of her bottom. She would look up at him as he relaxed on the veranda and smile without a chiding word. He sighed and looked down the gravel drive to the entrance that had long lost its wooden bar gate; another decline in his neglect.

He felt his daughter Julia tuck her arm in his just as the post girl arrived at the entrance to the drive.

She parked her red trolley, pulled out a couple of letters and began walking towards them. She was young with her light brown hair tied back in a pony-tail which swung from side to side as she bounced forward on the balls of her feet. She wore a tight red tee shirt which accentuated her full breasts and tight, black leggings which showed off her athletic legs.

'Hello, my dear,' Robert said as she neared. 'Got some cheques for me?'

She scrutinised the brown envelopes and smiled back. 'More like bills I'm afraid.' She passed over the mail and with a toss of her pony-tail she spun round and began walking back down the drive.

Robert and his daughter watched her go. 'My word,' Robert uttered under his breath, 'what an active bottom she has.'

'Father!' the voice of his other daughter, Celia, came from just behind him. 'That comment is unbecoming, especially at your age.'

Julia released her father's arm and turned back to her sister. 'You know, Celia, when you die they'll inscribe on your headstone: "Returned, unopened."'

Robert stifled a smile and Celia flinched at the rebuke. 'And your coffin will be Y shaped to allow for your legs to be permanently open as in life.' She realised she had spoken too quickly and she had faltered in her delivery and her voice was wrong and her attempted jibe failed, as usual. Her face reddened and she whirled round and went back into the house. Julia laughed and relinked her arm with her father.

'You know,' he said softly, 'you shouldn't tease your sister like that. Despite being your elder, she's never had the wit to match you. Besides, she'll probably burn the lunch now. Ah, this looks like Marcus has arrived.'

A black Volvo saloon eased through the entrance and crunched softly up the gravel drive towards them. Marcus cut the engine and got out of the car. Julia ran towards him and planted an over amorous kiss on his cheek; Robert, his uncle, came forward more slowly but his hug was just as warm.

'Good to see you Marcus,' Robert said, releasing him. 'You are welcome to stay as long as you like.'

Marcus smiled at the pair of them. 'Just a couple of days, I'm afraid. I wish it could be longer but I have still to work to earn the pennies.'

Julia took his arm and led him into the house. 'You stay however long you wish. We have made up a spare bedroom for you.'

Celia coughed, 'Well, I did actually.' She came forward and awkwardly gave Marcus a hug, half turning her face away. 'Lunch will be ready in thirty minutes. I hope you are hungry; I have prepared roast chicken with roasted potatoes. It used to be your favourite meal.'

'And still is,' Marcus lied; his culinary choice from

the times of being a small boy had widened and he would have accepted Italian pasta or an Indian curry or Mexican with chillies; but he said nothing, pleased alone to be in the company of his uncle and his two daughters.

Lunch was a question and answer time; Robert and Julia brought him up to date on their situation; although now retired, Robert had his own personal income and had little to reveal as his life centred on the village and there was not much life in the village. Julia mentioned, without enthusiasm, that she worked locally and as her father had said, there was not a lot going on locally. She had to travel down to the larger towns if she wanted any night life.

Celia, noticeably, had nothing to add to the conversation. Marcus told them about the 'special project' he was working on and fortunately, no one raised the subject in the headlines about his forthcoming speech for the IDM.

After lunch, Robert led him into the lounge and made for the drinks table. 'Can I get you a drink? Bourbon was your favourite, I recall?'

'Actually, a beer will be good.'

'I'll get it,' Celia said quickly and disappeared into the kitchen to retrieve a cool bottle from the refrigerator.

'And one for me,' Julia shouted after her. When Celia returned, she handed a bottle to Julia and then went to the table and poured Marcus's beer into a glass. 'There,' she said, handing the glass to him. 'You do not appear the type to drink it straight from the bottle; a bad habit.' She glanced pointedly towards Julia who just raised her bottle to her with a smile and then drank from it.

Robert ignored his daughter's rival banter and poured himself a large Scotch and raised his glass. 'Glad to have you with us, Marcus.'

Robert challenged Marcus to a game of chess out on the rear veranda. They settled in their chairs and Robert set up the pieces. For once, Julia had offered to help Celia to clear the table and wash up.

'Would I be right in guessing your visit has a purpose?' Robert enquired.

Marcus smiled. 'It's nothing drastic, uncle. Just a few things happening and I wanted to get away for a few days.'

Robert had given himself the white pieces and made the first move with a central pawn; he leaned back and took out a cigar and lit it. 'Celia makes hell if I smoke in doors; like her mother in that respect.' He drew lovingly on the cigar and blew a cloud of blue smoke towards the garden. 'She's a good girl and looks after me and the house but I wonder if she will ever find a man who would put up with her ways.'

Marcus moved a pawn to counter Robert's move. 'By 'her ways' I assume you mean her desire to run everything.'

'Yes, God help the man she does manage to talk into marriage; but somehow, unfortunately, I don't think that will happen.' He brought out a knight.

'She is not bad looking,' and then Marcus slightly corrected himself, 'she doesn't have Julia's beauty but I'm sure some bloke will...' He broke off as Celia brought them two coffees and put the cups with saucers on the table besides the chess board; Celia tutted to show her disapproval of Robert smoking a cigar but said nothing.

They thanked her and she returned into the house. 'That is what I mean,' Robert said, 'most girls would have made the coffee in mugs but she has to get out the best china; cups with saucers.'

Marcus found it amusing but his uncle was right. They made several more moves before Robert made his enquiry again. 'So, what are these few problems? Can you talk about them?'

Marcus paused for a moment, pretending he was studying the board; he was not sure how to broach the matter.

'It's my brother, your father, isn't it?' Robert said first.

Marcus sighed, 'Partly. I expect you saw in the newspaper that I have agreed to make a speech at the Independent Democratic Movement's conference. It made the headlines.'

'I saw them,' Robert smiled. 'Did he ring you and shout down the phone how much you were betraying him and his position?'

'Actually, I went to see him on Friday. I felt I owed him that much to tell him in person.'

'And so he shouted to your face.'

'Pretty much; he said I was betraying him as you said and took it personally. Of course, he was right but it was the way he attacked me without asking first, why I was doing it. I realise now it was a waste of time.'

Robert puffed another cloud of blue smoke and moved a bishop. 'You said you had a few problems; are they for the same reason?'

'Partly; my boss wants me to work from home, which is easy enough, but his reasoning is that he doesn't want his firm caught in the middle of a media storm. I can see his view but I had not thought about the consequences of making the speech once it became known. That was an error on my part.'

Robert hummed and planned his next move. 'At least he is letting you continue work. Some would have suspended you.'

'He is a good man, I appreciate that and it makes it harder for me that I am letting him down but I must make this speech.'

Robert said, 'Your move, you're in check. Tell me why you want to make the speech; is it simply to get at your father?'

'Not entirely; I do really believe in what the IDM want to achieve. I think the days of party politics must end. It has always been divisive but over the past few years, particularly through the Brexit debacle, it has been exposed to deceit, lies, betrayals and a new type of autocracy, especially since my father became PM.' Marcus paused.

'It was something that Sir Rees Lipton said that really made me think. He said there was no point in an opposition party. They were ineffective without a vote that could change the course of a government. For a period of five years, several hundred MP's were ineffectual and could only voice their opinions.'

'And important opinions; without their opposition, there would be no check and balance.'

'But Sir Rees is quite right. No matter how many seats the opposition parties have, it is a fact that they don't have a vote. An effective vote, that is.' Marcus looked up from the chess board, 'I'm sorry, uncle. I did not mean to become a preacher.'

Robert smiled, 'That is okay, I admire your enthusiasm. However, you are still in check.'

Marcus played out of it but without his mind totally focussed on the game, his uncle had him 'mate' within a few more moves. Robert leaned back and chuckled and then got up and went into the house, returning shortly with two glasses of

Bourbon in his hands. He handed one to Marcus and sat down. 'I have never beaten you so easily. In fact, I rarely have beaten you, so tell me; are there other matters?'

Marcus sipped and then said, 'There is a woman in the IDM; she's head of Administration and well, to be honest, we have had a relationship. My fiancée, Kate, has been suspicious for a while and on Friday, she saw a text from this girl, on my phone and left; leaving her ring behind. I have tried to call her but she won't answer.'

'And why did you have this affair?'

Marcus sought for an answer but the truth either eluded him or he was not prepared to face it. He took a deep breath and realised he could not keep it hidden inside where it would gnaw away at his conscience.

'She is just so beautiful. Really uncle, I have never come across a woman like her.' He paused looking for the right words. 'She made it clear she wanted me and I guess I could not resist.'

'You said 'woman'. Does that mean she is older than you?'

'Yes, but not that much. I seem to be making several errors of judgement lately.'

Robert watched his nephew for a moment. 'So Kate is really the girl you want?'

'I always thought so but how could I let myself

be led on by this other woman? It is making me question everything.'

'And what about the IDM; have you thought about its future?'

'I do not intend to stand as a member at an election; if that is what you mean. I just believe it is what we need to govern this country. Once I have made the speech, I shall quietly withdraw.'

Robert sighed. 'If they let you,' he mused. 'I have thought about its future and do like the idea. But suppose at an election, it gains a majority in the House; it could not function properly with the old style parties still around. Parliament could not survive a hybrid system.'

'I would hope it would gain a big enough majority to overcome a party system.'

'By banning parties; that would be a massive step. And let's just suppose Parliament was made up of all independents; how long would that survive before groups gathered into pacts to get their ideas through and before you know it, there would be a pseudo party system again.'

Marcus shook his head, 'I must admit I had not thought that far ahead. Hopefully, with a parliament made up only with Independents, they would embrace the freedom of free thinking.'

'That's a big wish,' Robert said. 'And of course, there are many other matters like the economy and foreign policies and law and order. Where do they stand? I haven't read much about their views on those issues.'

'There is something else,' Marcus said. 'I have attended several meetings now and at one of them a Professor of Economic and Business Psychology gave a speech about the difference between need and want. At the lower financial end, people have more of a need for food, housing and clothing. They want a better life but their needs outweigh the want because that is out of reach until the needs are satisfied. The very rich on the other hand have all their needs satisfied but their wants increase as desires for more. For example, a rich tycoon will have a big house or several and perhaps a fleet of cars and then, because another has a yacht, he has a want for a yacht of his own but probably even bigger.'

Marcus paused and looked at Robert who nodded to show he was following him so he continued. 'When he becomes a millionaire or a billionaire his need does not exist so he replaces the need he knew when he had little money, to a want. The question he never asks himself is: how much money can one spend in a lifetime. Do you understand that?'

Robert nodded. 'Yes. It is quite true but one always needs a motivation in life. If you do not have much money then you need more to buy the things you need and if you have plenty you seek

ways of spending it. It's all about life improvement depending upon what your values in life are.
There are many very rich people who have become philanthropists and use their wealth to help others.'

'Very true,' Marcus agreed, 'and the IDM philosophy is not by robbing the rich to give to the poor but to redistribute personal wealth.'

Robert chuckled, 'Is there a difference?'

'I'm sorry; I have not explained it well. The idea is not to strip the wealthy of their wealth but to control how much personal income we can earn. It will stop board members of companies awarding themselves huge salaries and bonuses because of their positions rather than their value to a company.'

Robert relit his cigar and puffed out more smoke. He shook his head slowly, 'That sounds an extremely complicated measure to introduce and then enforce.'

Marcus felt his own inadequate explanation had failed to impress his uncle; it sounded sensible when the Professor had explained it. Robert did not make a further comment on that subject, and instead he decided to address the problem of his brother.

'One thing I want you to understand; regarding your father. He is the elder of us and even as small children, he was a bully. He put me through some trying times. As he grew up he became a less physical bully but became a mental bully. He was arrogant and forced himself upon others. He never accepted contrary views and would shout down dissenters. I avoided him as much as I could and eventually, stopped seeing him altogether. I felt very sorry for your mother. I don't know what she saw in him as she was so different. She was quiet but more, she had a brain. She was a thinking woman with two degrees in classics and philosophy, as you well know. Perhaps it was his charisma; I really don't know. But what I do know is that after you were born, she regretted him and devoted herself to you.'

'I do know that,' Marcus said slowly.

Robert sighed. 'You may think I am out of order saying this but I am his brother and I feel I can say it, even to you. I understand how you feel and why you are doing what you are doing. You have my support and anything I can do to help, well, you just have to ask.'

Marcus reached across and touched his uncle's arm. 'Thank you, uncle. I am aware of what sort of man he is and he will not bully me from doing what I think is right.'

'Getting back to politics, there is another thing that I have pondered upon. The IDM wants to get rid of the Party system, but what about the House of Lords? Is it their intension to abolish it?'

Marcus thought for a moment. 'Why would they take such a step?'

'I can think of many but firstly, the Lord's is

divided by Party politics. Would it be the IDM's intention to ban party politics there too? I mean, you couldn't have a free Commons but a tied Lords.'

Marcus smiled. 'I haven't thought about that and nobody has talked about it.'

'Well, it will become a serious issue if the Commons House is non-party. Has anyone mentioned about not needing a second house. I mean, if the Commons is full of free thinkers then what will be the role of the Lords?'

'I shall ask about that next time I am back with the IDM people.' He thought for a moment. 'That's a very interesting point.'

'Sorry to stir the grey matter. It has always been a hobby horse of mine. It always rubbed me the wrong way to think that some people have so much responsibility but with nothing more than antiquated privilege.' Robert laughed aloud. 'Here ends the first lesson.'

Marcus smiled. 'An interesting point though. I shall certainly make enquiries.'

'My advice is to say nothing and just keep your ears to the ground. It could be a very contentious issue and that is why people in the IDM are avoiding the subject.'

Marcus nodded. 'So you think we could govern without a House of Lords?'

'It's an old chestnut. They are at best a delaying

tactic. Perhaps a second House is needed but again, like the Commons, it should be elected.' Robert shrugged. 'But if the Commons is non-party then so should the Lords, or whatever they want to call it.'

Marcus mused upon this; he was learning so much just from this evening chat with his uncle; he realised he still had so much more to learn.

'It is my intention that once I have made the speech, be it successful or not, I will concentrate on my work as an architect. I have no desire to be involved in politics, certainly not as a member of the House.'

Robert puffed unsuccessfully on his dead cigar. He lit it again and when satisfied with a blue, grey cloud rising to the air, he spoke again. 'I am pleased to hear that. You have a good career and future in front of you. As long, that is, you get your heart sorted out.'

Marcus sighed; over dinner he had hinted at a problem with Kate and another woman who worked for the IDM. Julia had immediately homed in on this but Marcus had refused to enlarge on the subject. Now he wondered what would be the more difficult; getting Kate back or releasing himself from Diana's grasp?

By the end of the day, Marcus felt exhausted, mainly from his inner conflict, and excused himself early and retired to bed. He had, since the release of the news about his forthcoming speech, switched off his mobile phone after it became hot with calls from the Press. He switched it on as he lay in his bed and had to plough through reams of missed calls, all from unknown numbers and presumably from the Press. There was no call from Katie. He switched off the phone and nestled down in the covers, trying to equally switch off his mind.

It was much later, when the house was quiet, that Marcus stirred. He was aware of someone next to him in the bed and a hand caressing him between his legs. He rolled over, switched on the light and looked to his left; Julia's face grinned back at him.

'What....what are you doing here?' he managed a hoarse a whisper. Even just coming out of a sleep, he was sensible enough to realise the situation and did not want the embarrassment of his uncle finding him in bed with his daughter.

Julia laughed quietly and moved closer, reaching again for him but he pushed her hand away. 'Now stop that and get out. My God, what if your father caught us together?'

'But I can tell you want me here,' She reached for him again and managed to clasp him this time. 'You see how big you are; you like it.'

Marcus again pushed her hand away and sat up. 'Please! Julia! We can't do this. Please leave and go back to your bed.'

Julia suddenly disappeared beneath the sheets and moved her head towards him like a shark honing in on its prey but he slid out of the bed and stood naked for a second before retrieving his boxer shorts and putting them on. 'Enough,' he said in a harsh whisper. Julia sat up in the bed with a disapproving pout on her lips but at the same time, allowing her breasts to be exposed and tempt him further.

'Come back, Marcus. Just for a cuddle. I was getting so lonely in my bed, especially knowing you were here, alone as well.'

Marcus moved quickly round the bed and pulled the sheets back revealing she was totally naked and pulled Julia's arm and lifted her out of the bed. She squealed and Marcus was afraid his uncle would hear. 'Go back to your bed,' he whispered, opening the door and pushing her through with a final slap on her buttocks as he closed the door.

The next morning, Marcus was awoken by the village church bells to remind him where he was and it was Sunday morning. He wondered if anyone, particularly his uncle, had heard Julia's visit to his room but at breakfast, his uncle said nothing and seemed unaware of the night's escapade. Celia however, bided her time with a knowing look on her face.

Finally she asked Marcus, 'Did you sleep well, Marcus. I heard a bit of noise in the night. I'm sure it was from your room.'

'Just a dream, I think. I sometimes talk in my sleep,' he looked pointedly at Julia.

'My sister often causes nightmares,' Celia said, buttering some toast with a demure look on her face.

Julia looked back at both of them with a sweet smile on her lips.

After breakfast, Marcus put on his coat and told them he was going for a walk; he wanted some time to think things over. Robert suggested he follow the road to the end and climb over a stile gate and follow a path up by the edge of a wood. It would lead him onto the hilltops and he would have a good view of the village.

Julia said, 'I'll join you. I could do with a bit of exercise.'

'I think I need to be alone,' Marcus said, 'I have a few things to mull over.'

'Better to talk them over with someone than just mope about them,' Julia smiled sweetly, 'I'm a very good listener.'

Celia made a 'huh' noise but Julia ignored her and went for her coat.

Marcus and Julia linked arms and made their way down to the stile.

'What do you do? I mean what sort of job do you have?' Marcus asked her.

'Well, according to Celia I am the local harlot,' she

replied, 'I only work five days a week that's why I'm off for this weekend. Have to build my strength up for the next week.'

Marcus laughed. 'I'm sure if that were true, Celia would have made sure to tell me very quickly.'

'Actually, I run the Accounts department with the local dairy co-operative. It's a group of five dairies. It is very boring but pays well. I want to get out of here, perhaps find a job in London and find some life. Maybe you could put me up in your apartment while I get settled.'

'Now that would definitely not be a good idea.'

'My going to London or you and me sharing a flat?' she asked.

'Both.'

They arrived at the wooden stile and Marcus helped her over, noting she made the most of showing off her legs in a short skirt.

'So, tell me what it is you have to think about?' she asked as they made their way up the path alongside the wood.

'Where do I start and don't say at the beginning.'

'But where else should you start? Come on, I bet it's this woman or maybe more than one.'

Marcus looked sideways at her. 'Why do you suppose it has to be about a woman?' He paused and then added, 'Well, actually that is just one of the problems.'

'Then come on; tell Agony Auntie Julia everything.'

He took in a deep breath. 'I have or had a fiancée named Katie. But then I had an affair with this other woman and Katie found out, well not exactly found out, but she became suspicious.'

'But she was right, you were having an affair.'

Marcus sighed, 'In a way.'

Julia laughed out loud. 'There is only one way to have an affair. You were having rumpy-pumpy.'

'It wasn't as straight forward as that.'

'Oh, I see, it was a bit kinky as well,' Julia continued to laugh. 'I'm sorry Marcus but men always think that they are having just a harmless bit of fun when women think they are having an affair.'

Marcus smiled. 'Alright, it was an affair with all that goes with it. Except, and I have to emphasise this, I do not love her whereas I do love Katie.'

'So the next question is: if you love Katie, why were you tempted into an affair with another woman?'

'That I don't know. Yes I do,' he corrected himself immediately. He paused and Julia waited while he found the words. 'She, this other woman, is the most beautiful woman I have ever encountered and I suppose, I was so flattered by her attentions that I gave in to her temptations. There!' He seemed relieved that he had finally said it.

Julia stopped and clapped her hands. 'Well done, Marcus. You see, it's not so difficult to admit it when you face up to it.'

Marcus moved close and gave her a hug. 'Okay Agony Aunt Julia, what the hell do I do about it?'

She pushed him away but held onto his hands. 'Do you still love Katie and do you still want to marry her?'

'Yes, most definitely I do,' he admitted.

'Then it is simple. You stop this affair business, you go to Katie when you return to London and you tell her you have made a big, stupid mistake with someone who means nothing to you; you are sorry, and you love Katie and want to get married as soon as possible.'

Marcus thought about her advice. 'That simple; do you think it will work?'

'If she still refuses you then you know that she has thought things through and realised you are not the right one for her.'

'Oh.' Her words struck home and he knew he would remember them.

Julia moved closer and put her hands on his shoulders. 'I'm sorry Marcus but I have to be honest. Life can be a bitch.' She saw his face fall to sadness. 'Hey, she may still love you; in fact I bet she does. Come on,' she tugged at his arm, 'let's keep going to the top of the hill. The view is good.'

The hill was not very high and was rounded at the top and, as she had said, the view was good. Side by side there were two weather beaten benches; their varnish stripped and the wooden slats were dark with age. They ignored the benches and looked down to the village which looked like a model with miniature houses, a pub and a church and tiny cars made their way round the defined roads. Julia stood behind him and put her arms round his chest and hugged him close.

'It'll all work out, Marcus, you'll see.'

He smiled but more from hope than belief, 'I'm sure it will.'

'Of course, if you need any more comfort, especially tonight, I can always come and give you a cuddle.'

He turned so that he could put his arms around her and hugged her more tightly, 'You're a little minx. You never give up,' he laughed.

'Would you expect me to?'

Marcus shook his head. 'No, I guess not. That wouldn't be you.'

'And now,' she added, 'are there any other problems I can help you with?'

Marcus looked deep into her eyes and held her stare for a moment. 'They are only problems that I can resolve. In fact, I think they may be beyond resolving.'

'Is this the business about you making a speech?'
'Quite.'
'Simple again, you don't make the speech.'
'No, it is not that simple, I have to. It is not just that I have said I would; I want to make it. The problem is it should have remained a secret until the day I made it but somebody leaked it and I have a good idea who.'

'Would it be the fair maiden with whom you shared pillow talk?' She dug her hands into the deep pockets of her coat and took out a packet of cigarettes and a lighter and lit one, puffing the smoke into the light breeze.

'I didn't know you smoked?'

She grinned, 'There are a lot of things you don't know about me. And,' Julia added, 'nor does Celia so don't go snitching on me.'

'Of course not,' he promised.

'Now, about this fair maiden, do you suspect her?'

'It could be. It is one of two people I suspect. There is also the Chairman of the Movement. I thought he was a pretty straight type but I just have a feeling that he and Diana, that's the girl, may have been colluding.'

Julia took one more puff on the cigarette and then threw it on the ground and trod on it. 'If I was you, I would let it go.'

'You would; why?'

'Simple my dear Marcus; they will deny it, you cannot prove it and it will achieve nothing. You want to make the speech so go on, write it and make it.'

Marcus smiled, 'I wish my life was as simple as yours. Hey, the time is getting on; we had better walk back.'

She fished in her pocket, took out a bag of mints and popped one in her mouth. 'That's to stop Detective Celia smelling my smoking,' she explained. She linked her arm in his and they made their way down the hill. 'My life is not that simple, Marcus, I am restive. I need to move on; find the niche I need.'

'Perhaps it's a fella.'

'That would be simple. No, I really do need to get away from this environment. Daddy is great but my life is stagnating in this place.'

'Well, the world is your oyster, as they say.'

'That is an awful expression and besides, I'm no pearl.'

They returned to the house in time for Celia to announce lunch would be ready in fifteen minutes. She also made some comment about the effort it had taken while others enjoyed a 'romp' on the hills but they had turned away and ignored her. Marcus found his uncle in the drawing room, seated in an armchair and reading the Sunday paper.

'I suppose they are full of me and my making a speech?'

Robert lowered the paper to look at him. 'Naturally but they seem to be on your side. At least they have no idea where you are. They think you have secreted yourself away so your father can't get at you.'

'It's not on my side that I want them. I want them to understand why. If I had made the speech before they knew, then the reason would have been clear.'

'I have thought about that; who may have leaked it, I mean.' His uncle got up and went over to the drinks on the sideboard. 'Shall I pour a glass of Bourbon for you?' Marcus assented and his uncle poured one for him and a scotch for himself. He handed Marcus his glass. 'That will warm you up after your walk. Where is Julia, by the way?'

'I think she went straight to her room; probably to change. So what is your idea about the leak?'

Robert returned to his seat and tasted his scotch and waited for Marcus to settle in the seat opposite him.

'There are two possibilities. The first is your father but one must ask; why would he when on the surface it would do him no good? But think about it; if you made the speech without warning then the impact might be all the greater. By getting it out now, how long before it became old news and forgotten?'

'But it would be resurrected when I make the speech. That is only a few weeks away,' Marcus queried. 'Surely that is asking for double the trouble.'

His uncle said, 'Yes,' slowly. He had thought about that obviously and he came back with, 'But it would be expected and not a sudden surprise. I know my brother; it would give him a few weeks to play it down and I'm sure he would come up with something. I suspect he may even go in for a bit of character assassination.'

'Of me? His son?' Marcus queried; somewhat surprised by that.

'He's quite capable. You said he took it badly when you told him, well, it would be typical of him to come out fighting even at your expense.'

Marcus thought about this and he had to admit, his father was more than capable of sacrificing his own son for his own salvation. 'Putting that aside, that leaves only one alternative. Someone in the Movement made the leak. I suspect it to be more likely but I'm not sure why they would do it?'

'Well, there could be a few reasons for that,' Robert emptied his glass and got up and went over to the sideboard to refill it. 'The first thing I thought of is that by making it public, they would ensure you made the speech.' He returned to his chair. 'You would lose face if you decided not to; perhaps they are a bit concerned that you may have a change of heart.'

'It is more probable that I would refuse if I found out they had deliberately leaked it.'

'Possibly, but how could you prove someone inside the Movement had? No, they will deny it and they have stolen a march with the publicity. Now everyone, or at least the media, will be counting down to your speech. They will fan the flames with speculation about what you are going to say.'

Marcus swallowed his bourbon in one gulp. 'I know it is too late but I wish I had never agreed to it.'

Robert sat forward. 'Did they suggest it? I thought you volunteered. That puts a different light on it.' He looked intently at his nephew. 'Marcus, are you sure you know what you are getting in to? Was it one particular person who persuaded you?'

Marcus wanted to get himself another drink but at that moment, Celia came in and announced lunch was on the table.

Robert stood up. 'We'll talk more after lunch,' he said. 'You may not like it but I think we ought to discuss this more.' Then, as Marcus stood, he clapped him on the shoulder. 'Come on, let's put it to one side for the moment and enjoy whatever Celia has cooked up.' As they went to the dining room, he added, 'Her one, and perhaps only attribute is her fine cooking.' He laughed away his detrimental remark about his own daughter.

That evening Marcus retired early to lie on his bed and turn over the many problems that beset his mind. He tried to phone Katie several times but her phone was switched off. Eventually he gave up and stripped off and after a quick wash and cleaning his teeth, he got into bed. Sleep came quickly and against his expectation, Julia did not sneak between his covers in the wee hours.

In the morning, he awoke and lay for a while with his eyes open; through the night while perhaps dreaming of better things, his brain had beavered away in his sub-conscience and untangled the twisted strands that had fuelled his anxiety. He knew what he wanted to do.

He got up, showered and dressed and went down the stairs with a lighter heart. Celia was in the kitchen and she looked up and smiled as he entered.

'A quieter night?' she enquired with just a hint of a smile.

It made Marcus wonder if she lay awake all night listening for her sister's adventurous escapades. 'I slept very well,' Marcus said, 'Am I the first up?'

'No, Julia has gone to work and father is pottering about somewhere. I'm just preparing his breakfast; he likes a cooked breakfast. Can I do one for you?'

Surprisingly, with his lightened mood, Marcus was hungry and asked for the same.

While she prepared the eggs and bacon meal, Celia asked, 'Are you leaving today

'No, I would like to stay for a few days. I hope you and your father will be okay with that.'

'I'm sure it will be alright. Here's a coffee; black no sugar,' she said as she put a cup with a saucer on the table.

Marcus suppressed a smile and sat at the table just as his uncle came in to the kitchen. 'I heard that, it's fine for you to stay as long as you like actually. We're glad to have you here, right Celia?'

'Of course, father. Sit down, here is your breakfast,' she put a plate of fried eggs, bacon and sausages on the table. 'And here's yours Marcus. Toast is just coming.'

Marcus noted the way Celia always called him 'Father' whilst Julia called him 'Daddy'. Was it just a term of endearment or did it reveal the different characters of the two girls. Whatever, it didn't matter and he tucked into his food with relish.

'So, why do you want to stay a few days?' Robert asked, feeding a fork of sausage into his mouth.

'I have decided what I am going to do. About everything,' he added. 'I shall make the speech, I shall sort out this business of the leak and I will see Katie and sort our relationship as well.'

Robert sipped his coffee. 'That's good; you sound more positive. Sometimes it's best to sleep on a problem.'

Marcus reached for a slice of toast from the rack Celia had put on the table. 'That is exactly what happened. I drifted off to sleep last night with all the problems of the world and this morning I awoke with the solutions.'

Robert looked keenly at him. 'I hope they all work out.'

Marcus looked at his uncle and his expression slightly changed. 'I'll have to see, I guess,' he said softly and with less enthusiasm. 'Whatever the outcomes, I shall have to cope.'

'Good; just remember that you are in charge,' Robert said and then added. 'As we used to say in the army: 'Don't let the buggers win'.'

'I had forgotten you served,' Marcus said.

'Five years for Queen and country; that was a waste. Thought I would make a career of it as an officer but I could never get used to not arguing with someone of a higher rank than me who was wrong.'

'And you always like a good argument, don't you,' Celia smiled.

'A good discussion,' Robert corrected her.

Marcus spent the two days working on an idea for the speech and going for solitary walks while he further mulled over his thoughts; it was not a matter of how much he wanted to say but what it was he wanted to convey. Too much and his message would be lost in the words and people's attention span and he struggled to find the right medium.

For a break, he drove Celia to a nearby town which offered a large supermarket so she could stock up with more food. When they had loaded the bags in his car, he treated Celia out for lunch; a way to repay her for looking after him. He played chess several times with his uncle and beat him each time, which assured him he was in a better frame of mind. Early on his final evening, he went for a walk into the village with Julia; partly for the exercise and also to bounce a few ideas passed her to see what she thought.

He linked his arm in hers as they walked. 'I'm going to make the speech but I shall keep it a secret until I make it. No more leaks.'

'Good thinking,' Julia concurred. 'I'm glad you are going to make it. Daddy was keen you would.'

Marcus looked at her. 'So he discussed it with you?'

Julia squeezed his arm with hers. 'Of course he did. Daddy has been thinking about it and always chats to me about his ideas. Does that bother you?'

'No, of course not; I suppose I should have guessed he would. You are very close with him. Are you so sure you want to move away?'

They had arrived in the village main street and Julia avoided his question and uncoupled their arms. 'I'm just popping into this shop to get some more fags.'

'Do you really want to?' he asked.

She stuck her tongue out at him before

disappearing into the shop. When she reappeared she was already opening the packet and he waited while she lit it and drew deeply on it before exhaling a dense cloud. He decided it was pointless to say anything.

'You know,' she said, 'I think it is far more important that you sort out your relationship with your fiancée and this other piece, Diana is it, before you try to put together your speech. I mean, the speech is important and everyone, the Press, TV and your father of course; will all be watching so it is important you get it absolutely spot on.' She paused while she took another long pull on the cigarette. Marcus waited as she turned to him.' It is the moment in your life. I mean it. Do you want me to help with it?'

Marcus smiled, 'Thank you but no; this has to be me; from my heart, so to speak.'

Julia shrugged as they continued walking, they did not link arms as he wanted a short distance away from the clouds of smoke issuing from her lips. She finally flipped the cigarette into the gutter and ground it under her heel.

'Shall we pop into the Bull for a quick one before we go back for dinner?' she asked but was already heading across the road towards the pub.

'Alright,' said Marcus as he followed her, 'but just one. You may enjoy upsetting Celia but I don't want a burnt offering.'

Later, when they had returned, Celia excelled with roasted pork with crispy crackling, homemade apple sauce and sauté potatoes. This was followed by an ice cream mountain with raspberries covered in a whipped cream. Robert insisted at the end that they all, including a reluctant Celia, had a glass of brandy to toast Marcus's success with his forthcoming speech.

When they all finally made their way to bed, Julia followed Marcus to his door and looked at him with doe like eyes. 'Last chance,' was all she said.

Marcus smiled and kissed her lightly on the lips. 'Let's not complicate things,' he said quietly and went into his room.

On his way back to London, Marcus stopped off at a shopping centre and bought food, almost randomly, so that he could stock his larder and fridge and avoid having to go out locally where he might have been seen.

He drove to the rear of his apartment block to the courtyard where the residents had their own parking spaces marked out. He entered the building from the rear entrance and walked up the stairs to his floor. He paused on the landing but there was no one about so he quickly went to his door and let himself in.

He unpacked the things he had bought into the fridge and cupboards and then unpacked his suitcase. The pile of used clothes in the washing basket was enough for him to put them in the washing machine; this included a pair of Katie's panties which he found entangled with his own underwear.

He made himself a coffee and then went into his 'office' where he got out his draft drawings and notes for the 'Lakeland' project. When he had it all set up he paused and then went to the kitchen where, on the table, he had put the notes he had started to draft for his speech. He sat and started to read through them when his mobile phone rang. He did not recognise the number and was in two minds whether to answer or not; it could be the Press. In the end, he pressed the receive button. He was surprised to hear Katie's voice.

'Before you ask, I have bought a new phone. I had a couple of calls from the Press and decided to get a new number. I expect you may have tried to call me and was probably wondering why my phone appeared to be switched off.'

Marcus hesitated, 'Yes, actually I did try to call you a few times. I have been staying with my Uncle Robert. Do you remember him? He's my father's brother.'

She did not answer his question but instead said, 'I

think we should meet and get everything sorted out. I shall be in the Bluebell Café at six tonight.'

'The Bluebell?' he queried.

'Yes, the one near my work; we have been there.'

Marcus did remember it. It was a very basic café and he was surprised she was suggesting it but he supposed she found it easy to get to. He shrugged mentally, 'Okay, I'll see you there at six.' The call was ended by Katie without another word.

The call put him off kilter and for the rest of the afternoon, he wandered about his apartment, picking one minute at the project and the next, going to the kitchen and reading his speech notes. He decided to have a shower to pass some more time and eventually the clock managed to drag its hands to five-thirty and he phoned for a taxi as he knew parking would be impossible in that area near the Bluebell café.

He went in, ordered himself a straight black coffee and sat at a table. Katie joined him within a minute which suggested to him that she had probably been waiting across the road, waiting to see him arrive first. She refused the drink he offered to get.

She was dressed in a sloppy grey jumper that hid her figure and an old pair of grey jeans. Her hair looked dull and was pulled back tightly into a bun; she wore little or no makeup. To Marcus she seemed to have made herself as unattractive as possible. He did not feel confident.

Katie took in a deep breath and then spoke in a rehearsed manner. 'I have given a lot of thought to what has happened between us over the past few months. I think you have become obsessed with your job, obsessed with this IDM thingy and obsessed with this woman Diana. That is a lot of obsession, Marcus.' He thought he would speak but she hurried on. 'Considering we were planning to get married, I think you have shown quite clearly, that you are not, at this time, ready for marriage.'

She paused but he said nothing; Julia's words were filling his mind.

'So, I have decided, after a lot of thought, that I am not ready to be married. To you,' she added. She tilted her head to one side, 'I assume from your silence that you concur with me.'

He found his voice, 'Actually, I came here with the intention to apologise about my behaviour and how I have been treating you. I am sorry; truly sorry...'

She cut him off. 'You did not tell me where you were going off and I have used the time to think things through. I realise now that I do not love you, Marcus.' She stood up and looked down at him. 'I do not think we are suited.'

Dumbfounded and without knowing why, he held out a paper bag he had been carrying. She stared at it, took it and opened it.

'Your panties,' he said, 'I found them in the wash.'

Katie made a low growling noise in her throat and spun round and virtually ran out of the café. Through the café window, he watched her leave; she was hurrying across the road, almost running away from him. That was the last image he would have of her.

A young girl stood by his table. 'Your coffee,' she said putting a mug on the table and drifted away.

CHAPTER FOUR
WHEN THE DOGS ARE RELEASED

The Prime Minister had a meeting with the heads of some of the Trade Unions. They had been calling for a meeting for a while but he had deferred until he needed them. Now he had called them together to plead MacDonald's case but had decided not to include his Chancellor whose style and dry expressions often rankled rather than calmed their demeanour. Besides, at an earlier meeting with the PM, the Chancellor had implied that the Unions were in a desperate financial state after a series of strikes and while they may adopt an aggressive stance, it was unlikely they wanted to follow through with their threat of more industrial actions.

But this meeting did not go well; they listened in silence while he put forward his case but when he had finished they seemed to line up and take cues from each other. He guessed rightly that they had prepared for him and they hit him with strong arguments with the rolling rattle of a Gatling gun. At last he sat back, exhausted from having his every point blunted and rejected.

'Alright, so tell me, what is it you want?'

Ballard, who was leading the group, leaned forward with his large hands clasped in an aggressive manner. 'When you first took over you promised us if we held back on any actions like strikes, then you would have time to get the economy straight and the working man would be the first to benefit.' He looked around at his colleagues. 'We're still waiting. Next, get rid of MacDonald. He has lost the plot and we,' he looked along the line of faces, 'feel his cock-eyed plan was wrong from the start. We want Philip Milner to take his place.'

The PM sat stunned for a moment; he felt this was an indirect rejection of himself as he had always backed MacDonald's economic strategy; in fact he had sat with him for hours putting it together. Secondly, Milner was a new boy; a recognised economic expert but of the new school who had been loudly vocal in his criticism of the Chancellor's plan, especially when it had first slowed and then showed the signs of stripping apart. Milner would change the whole strategy and more important, he wasn't one of the three and he would fight against the PM's hands on approach. But the final barb was the very fact that the Unions were dictating to him who he should hire and fire.

'I cannot accept that,' he said slowly, 'Archie has been struggling against abnormally adverse conditions but I know he is working on that right now and will shortly be coming up with a new incentive that will get us back on track. I have always said that such a change in the structure of our economy would take time.'

'But for how long?' Ballard interrupted.

The PM raised his head and looked Ballard directly in the eyes. 'For as long as it takes. Look, these are precarious times. If you force my hand with more strike action then I shall have to go to the country and you could find you are meeting with a whole set of different people. Do you know what I mean?' Ballard did not respond but the PM could see from his eyes that the word 'Tories' was clearly etched and it frightened him. The PM nodded, 'Very well then, all I ask is for time. It shall work.' And then he repeated for emphasis, 'It shall work.'

Ballard hunched his shoulders. 'I'll say just this; we'll give you a while longer but only a little while. We've had many promises over the years from the Tories and the likes of you. One thing we don't have when it comes to our members pay and that is patience. If that Scottish friend of yours doesn't come up with something, and soon, we'll insist Milner replace him.'

The PM did not immediately trust himself to respond. He bided his time and then decided to put the ball back in Ballard's court. 'So, you obviously have a plan of your own, what is it?'

Ballard smiled; that was more like it. 'We have economist type fellows in our ranks, as you well know. It is our considered opinion that now is the time to get some of those millions back from the rich types who have not earned it.'

The PM was not a swearing man but at that moment, he could think of a few choice words. This was the second time that week the subject of taxing the rich was being mooted. He suspected that MacDonald had been opening a second front with a few of his cronies in the Unions. He lifted a pencil and read the maker's name on the side. 'Perhaps you could enlighten me on just how you propose to soak the rich without putting our economy into jeopardy.'

Ballard smirked. 'Are you implying that our economy is not in jeopardy already?'

The PM dropped the pencil. 'What I say, and this is not just from my own judgement but also from the Chancellor,' he paused and raised a hand to stop Ballard intervening, 'we have looked far beyond raising various taxes from those, who shall we say, can afford it, but on the knock on effect of taking that money, not just from the men who have it, but from the economy itself. That money is not just sitting in men's bank accounts. It is being constantly re-invested to bolster and increment industry.'

'Bollocks,' Ballard said aloud. 'I am surprised to hear you say that. What about their rich style of living? What about the large houses they live in with swimming pools and grand yachts in the harbours?'

'And who do they employ to build those houses and yachts?' the PM countered.

'And what happens to all the monies they secrete into off-shore, tax-free countries?' Ballard had his teeth gripped and would not let go. 'That's yours and my money they are piling up.'

The PM sighed heavily. This was one of those "yes they do, no they don't" arguments which had no ending. 'Look,' he said with finality. 'The Chancellor and I are in full agreement that now is not the time to introduce taxes at the higher level of income. It shall come, I can assure you. The Chancellor and I have been studying the case in depth. You will see, over the coming months that we shall be implementing a stepped approach what will begin to tax the higher earners but without causing a major shift in investment of the industries we are so dependent upon.'

The PM, had he been a man with a conscience, would have crossed his fingers at that moment. But he was not a man of conscience; he had lost that somewhere along the way to his premiership.

Ballard was for once lost for a response. Finally he said, 'Alright. If that is the case,' he looked around at his colleagues, 'we'll hold off for the time being. But we need to see results.' He paused and then added,

'Very soon.'

When he was being driven back to Number 10, the PM was smarting at his treatment from the Unions; particularly Ballard. Something was going on behind the scenes. He wondered if the unions were in secret collusion with Milner. If that were so, then he had better watch and listen for any whispers coming from Milner's corner.

The PM sat in his room in Number 10 and mulled over his mauling at the hands of the Unions. He had, when he attained power, revoked and revised many Union laws on the understanding that they would be responsible to him and support his vision for the working class. He felt they were now flexing their considerable muscles and the only way he could keep them with him, was to show his vision was not just a pipe dream.

The door opened and MacDonald bustled in without waiting to be shown in by the secretary. 'John,' he almost shouted, 'what is this I hear about a meeting with the Unions? Why did you exclude me? What is going on?'

His questions rattled off and the PM waited until he sat down. He held up a hand and patted the air to indicate MacDonald should calm down.

'I saw them on my own simply to keep the meeting short and under my control.' MacDonald made to speak but the PM continued, 'I wanted a meeting, not a conference. Now, the reason for the meeting was at their request to discuss our future economic strategy.' He held up his hand again as MacDonald tried to intercede. 'If you had been there with your knowledge, they would have got down to detailed technicalities but with me,' he laughed to lighten the mood, 'they knew I could only speak in broad terms.'

MacDonald chewed this over in his head and somehow, perhaps through the flattery, he saw some sense in it. 'So what was their gripe?' he asked acidly.

The PM briefly outlined the meeting but he smoothed over the serrated edges and did not mention their proposal for Milner. He also failed to mention his promise of taxing the higher levels; there was time to surreptitiously introduce this to MacDonald at a time of his choosing. The PM concluded with, 'How is your work going with the re-assessment?'

'I have identified areas we can save some money on and shuffle it around and with a little more borrowing we can get the incentive projects back on stream.'

'More borrowing?' the PM queried.

'Aye, but kept to a minimum. You see....'

'When will you have all this put together and we can go through it?'

MacDonald raised his large eyebrows; he didn't like the interruption. 'Well, a week, maybe two.'

'One week,' the PM said firmly. He clasped his hands together in a pyramid and smiled across the desk. MacDonald wondered what was coming. 'I have been putting together a plan which I think will not only meet with your ethical approval, but will also remedy your long term financial woes.'

'Oh yes?' MacDonald raised his head as if sniffing the air, 'a plan for what?'

'This is of course strictly between us. Toby must not know; he will blow a gasket when he hears so I want it well advanced before anyone apart from us knows. Not even anyone in your department.' He looked keenly at the Chancellor who nodded but who was mystified what could be so momentous.

The PM relaxed back in his chair. 'I want you to have a secret meeting with the First Minister of Scotland in a few weeks. You being a Scot will make you the ideal candidate to speak with him.' The Chancellor's eyes narrowed. 'My plan is that Scotland will hold a referendum for independence within the next six months.'

He put his hand up to stop MacDonald's interruption. 'They have been chafing against the bit for so long to have another referendum and successive governments have thwarted them but I want you to tell him that I shall agree and that we shall not make an effort to oppose it again. In fact, we shall pave the way to make it more acceptable.'

'You know my thoughts on it,' the Chancellor got in at last. 'I am a Scot and want to see independence but what on earth changed your mind? You have always been a strong opponent to it.'

'I can see two benefits,' the PM said quietly, he wanted his words to ease into the Chancellor's head. 'The first part and I shall insist on it, is the SNP will no longer sit in the House which will improve our majority which has been eroding since the IDM won seats at bi-elections and there are two more coming up. And of course, not forgetting the defections from the Tories as well as us and I hear that if we lose the bi-elections, there could be more.'

'That's true,' the Chancellor admitted, nodding, 'And they have their conference soon and that could give them more points in the polls. But you said there were two benefits to your plan.'

'I think the second will appeal to you even more. I want you to tell him that the number one priority for the Scottish government is closing the Faslane base on the Clyde and we shall back him.'

'Trident?' the Chancellor exclaimed.

'Precisely; now, you and I have always wanted to get rid of the Trident submarines and become a non-nuclear nation. And I believe from some polls, that a large portion of our electorate feel the same.' This was not true but the PM was passed having scruples about lying, even to his Chancellor. 'It is a lot of money with nothing to show for it. Now just think, what has to happen if Faslane closes?'

'We will have to find another base; probably Portland.'

'At great cost,' the PM said.

'A huge cost,' the Chancellor agreed.

'And the whole Trident project is due for revue next year. What better time to argue against renewing Trident when the cost of moving the base and replacing the existing submarines and missiles will be beyond our means. And, just think of the savings we shall make.'

The Chancellor lifted his head and stared into space for a moment as the tumbrils whirled figures through his mind before his head slowly lowered and his thin lips curled into a smile. 'Mind you, a year is long term. I need something now.'

'But if you know the long term benefits, you can pull them forward,'

'There are some big 'ifs' in there.'

'I don't think so. The Scottish First Minister will be licking his lips when you explain it all to him. I plan for you to secretly go up to Edinburgh when the IDM is holding its conference and everyone; especially the Media will be distracted by that.'

The Chancellor felt not all was quite right. 'You can be sure of that. But I'm thinking that perhaps it will carry more weight if you talk about this with the First Minister.'

'No,' the PM said quickly. 'I am watched by the Media too much especially with my son stirring them up. They would sniff around if they knew I was going for talks with the First Minister. There is a trade fair coming up in Edinburgh just when the IDM has its Conference. You can go there for a visit and just quietly arrange a meeting between you in private.'

The Chancellor nodded his head with agreement. 'Aye, that sounds sensible.'

'Now, I have a meeting with Toby.' The PM stood up to signify the meeting was over.

The Chancellor stood also, 'With Fennel, what's that old fool up to now?'

The PM smarted; the jibes between those two were undermining his control. 'Just Home Office matters. I expect you have plenty to be getting on with. One week,' he re-iterated, 'I need your plans in one week. And remember, secrecy is imperative.'

MacDonald made a groaning noise in his throat as he left but the PM ignored it and pressed his intercom. He heard his secretary's voice, 'Has the Home Secretary arrived yet?' he asked.

'He's just entered Downing Street.'

'Show him in as soon as he arrives.'

He sat in his chair but was far from relaxed; in the early days there had only been good news and he had been in full, confident control but now the news always seemed to be bad and he had to work hard to maintain stability. At least he now had the Chancellor firmly on his side and now he had to secure Fennel; that would be a lot easier.

He leaned back in his chair; for some reason he felt a soft calmness spread through him. He liked to manipulate people be they the highest or lowest; the exception for failure was his son. This did not bother him; he had the people who mattered and MacDonald and Fennel really did matter. All he had to do was pull the trigger when he wanted to fire a shot at something or someone.

Toby Fennel entered and the PM waved him to the chair in front of his desk. 'Toby, how are things going with you?' The PM remained seated.

Fennel smiled as he sat, 'Better than with Archie. I saw him leaving here. If his face was the weather, I would be building an ark.'

The PM could not help but smile, 'Very droll.' He looked at Fennel for a moment and let the smile disappear. 'What do you know about the IDM and don't tell me they are a political movement?'

'You mean; do we keep an eye on them.'

The PM nodded. 'Have you found anything, shall we say, not quite right and above board?'

Fennel became a little wary, he knew the PM probably had heard something, perhaps from the Intelligence Service and he was testing him to find out if his department was on the ball. 'We are keeping a quiet watch on them,' he said, trying to be vague and hoping the PM would give him a clue about what he knew.

The PM was well used to Fennel's ploys and was a master of the cat-and-mouse game. 'That means you have not heard of anything amiss.'

'Perhaps you could enlighten me,' a faint line of perspiration was forming on Fennel's lips.

'It has been brought to my notice that there may be, shall we say, some dark forces at work.' The PM spoke in an almost hushed voice to emphasise the implied importance.

'Have you anything specific? If you have then I shall look into it,' Fennel said, feeling uneasy that the PM may be a step ahead of him.

'I have been having talks with a person from the Security Force who have set up a small unit; just to keep surveillance, you understand, and he has brought certain things to my attention.'

'And who might this person be?' Fennel queried.

'I shall be having a word with him tonight. I will suggest that perhaps he should, in future talk with you. You should head up this operation.'

'That sounds good. And his name is?' Fennel persisted.

'He'll tell you everything, after I have spoken with him.' The PM got up and went over to the window and pretended to be looking out at something. He suddenly turned and saw Fennel was writing notes in a small booklet. 'I wouldn't keep notes about this. The IDM is posing a direct threat to our democracy and in particular, to our party; but we must tread carefully. If the Press got to hear that we are looking into the IDM they would have a field day.'

Fennel closed the notebook and slipped it into his pocket with a face like a schoolboy caught sucking on a lollipop in class. 'I shall undertake this personally,' he said, and then he asked, 'is the Chancellor in on this?'

The PM saw his chance to seal the Home Secretary's allegiance. 'No. I am entrusting it only to you.'

Toby Fennel smiled broadly. 'I agree; it will be sensible to keep it to ourselves.'

'Absolutely and now I have important work. Thank you Toby.'

Fennel hesitated. 'How do I contact him?'

'As I said, I shall be speaking with him and then I shall let you know to contact him.' The PM walked over and stood by Fennel so that his size was impressive. 'I must emphasise that your meetings with him will be highly secret.' And then he added, 'Toby.'

Toby Fennel sat for a moment relishing the PM using his first name; then he rose slowly and left the room. The PM unlocked the drawer to his left and took out the mobile phone.

CHAPTER FIVE
HARMONY AND DISHARMONY

Marcus had received a call from Sir Rees Lipton who invited him to lunch at his town house. He assured Marcus it was a straight forward meeting to review his speech at the Conference and there was no problem. Marcus still believed Sir Rees might have been the one who leaked him making a speech and saw this as an opportunity to ask him.

He arrived around noon and felt he was stepping back into a past era; a butler met him at the door and ushered him into a large drawing room where Sir Rees was seated at a large mahogany desk. Marcus suspected he was posing with a pen and note paper which he laid down with a sweep of his hand and stood to welcome him.

Marcus had to admit that Sir Rees Lipton was a very elegant man; not just in his appearance but his manner was gentle and warm.

'Thank you for coming, Marcus. I'm sure you are a busy lad,'

Marcus accepted the 'lad' label from him as he was so much older and it was said in an affectionate way. 'Thank you. I think I can guess why you wanted to see me and I can confirm; I have completed the first draft. But it is only a draft.'

'Do you have it with you and,' Sir Rees paused to smile disarmingly, 'are you prepared to let me have a sight of it? I will understand if you will not want to leave a copy.'

'I would rather not,' Marcus said and saw the opening he wanted, 'especially after the leak that I was going to make the speech.'

Sir Rees's face fell; his lips tightened. 'May I impart something personal?'

'Of course,' Marcus agreed.

'Let us sit,' Sir Rees indicated to two padded upright chairs either side of a small, circular table, 'Jameson, two whiskies, if you please.'

Marcus noted that he was just as polite and relaxed with the staff; he sat and waited for Sir Rees to sit also; 'It has troubled me that the leak occurred so quickly after I had agreed to do it.'

'Quite right,' Sir Rees said passionately, 'I felt terrible. I imagined you must suspect me. I was going to call you but you disappeared for a few days.'

'I felt I had to get away from the Press and my Chairman suggested I work away from the office.'

Sir Rees shook his head slowly. 'I understand and I am mortified it happened.' He paused while the butler placed a tray with a decanter, a small jug of water and two glasses onto the table. He waited until they were alone again. 'I have something to say and I hope you will not feel I am speaking out of place.' He poured two whiskeys and indicated for Marcus to help himself to water.

'I will take no offence,' Marcus said, trying to be as amicable as he could.

Sir Rees's words came slowly and hesitantly; 'I realise that you may have developed, shall I say, a friendship with Diana.'

Marcus sipped his whisky and nodded.

Sir Rees hesitated but then added, 'I am afraid that I think it was probably she who leaked the information. I have spoken with her and she denied it but while her words said no, her face told me otherwise.'

'I had my own suspicion. I think you may be right but I do not know why she would do it.'

Sir Rees sipped his own drink. 'I think it was an ill thought out idea.' He looked up towards the ceiling, 'I think Diana is a young, vibrant woman who, while being fully committed to our ideals, has some of her own as well.' He gave a polite cough; 'I am sure she believes that you could play an important role at our conference; more than we intended. I think she sees a role for you afterwards.'

He waited for Marcus to speak but Marcus bided his time. 'When it was first mooted that you could give a speech, I was cautious. I could see the merit but

I am, at the same time, wanting to avoid a direct and personal conflict with the Prime Minister. Do you understand what I am meaning?'

Marcus thought for a moment and then made a sudden decision. 'Perhaps it would help if you read the draft of my speech first,' Marcus offered. He reached in the inside pocket of his coat and took out a folded sheaf of papers. 'It is only a draft. Just some rough ideas.'

Sir Rees was surprised. 'Oh, well yes, I'm sorry but I was not expecting you to allow me to see it. Does that mean you have confidence in me? I hope so.'

Marcus smiled assurance. 'Read it, please. I need to have your views on it.'

Sir Rees Lipton took the papers and went over to his desk. He put on his half-lens reading glasses. 'Help yourself to another whisky, please.' He began to read.

Marcus sat and watched the older man's facial expression; hoping to gain an insight to his opinion but as he read, Sir Rees's face remained blank and favoured no emotion. He finally laid the papers aside and took off his glasses. He stood up and slowly moved around the desk and made his way over to his chair where he sat down.

'That is quite something. You have written it very well and I can see you have expressed from your heart. It appears more than just a few rough ideas.

I..... I knew there was a conflict between you and your father but.....'

Marcus became concerned. 'Do you think I have overplayed that aspect?'

Sir Rees looked across at him with a softening smile. 'No, you have expressed yourself so very well. I note that you do not refer to him directly but your persuasion leaves no doubt. I think that if you make that speech, you will have the whole conference on your side. It's quite a master stroke.' Then Sir Rees's face became serious. 'I realise this is only a draft and you will work further to, um, polish it up, so to speak. But it is good.'

'Thank you.'

'Now young man, I must emphasise that it is of the utmost importance that your speech remain a secret until you actually make it at the conference.' He stood and went over to the desk and picked up the papers. 'No one else and I mean no one; especially Diana, cannot be allowed to see it.' He passed the papers to Marcus. 'Keep it close to your person.'

'May I ask you something?' When Sir Rees nodded he continued. 'I feel there may be a rift between you and Diana; am I right?'

Sir Rees smiled and intertwined his fingers; 'Politics no matter what shade of colour you favour has and always will be the same. You enter with high ideals but very quickly you realise that most, not all mind, are driven by one thing; ambition!' He unclasped his hands and flapped them gently, 'And ambition sits on top of a pyramid of deceit, manipulation, divisiveness, hedonism and a lot more. If you think I exaggerate then spend a day in the House. And, I'm afraid; the IDM is becoming no different.'

Marcus was taken aback. 'I know that applies to some members but you said most.'

Sir Rees smiled and shook his head. 'Perhaps I should have said some members. I paint the picture a little too bleak. I have been in politics most of my life and I'm afraid that those that practice ambition; are usually those that hold sway.'

'And you say it is in the Movement, so soon?'

'We'll see. I look into the future and see one big problem.' He paused, touched his finger-tips together and then continued. 'I whole heartedly agree with the ideals of the Movement but with the freedom of the individual we shall lose the glue of party loyalty.'

'I thought that would be its strength.'

'To have the freedom of expression is one thing but it also conjures the temptation to think and work as an individual and that can lead to thinking inwards. By that I mean ambition.'

Marcus sorted through the words and meaning. 'I thought the strength of an Independent system was expression of the individual; away from party lines.'

'Perhaps; it is a new concept and I hope all embrace the fundamentals of it.' Sir Rees paused for a moment, looking up at the ceiling before looking down again and continuing. 'I ask myself the question: are members to be seen as delegates of the voters, bound to follow the will of their electorate or are they representatives elected to exercise their own judgement in any changing circumstances.'

Marcus thought for a moment. 'Surely, they are individuals and they will follow their own persuasion. They will be voted for by their constituents upon what they say and on that be elected by their constituents.'

'Perhaps so, perhaps so,' Sir Rees repeated, much to himself.

Marcus again thought upon Sir Rees's words; was the older man having second thoughts? 'But my original question was about Diana.'

'Ah, well that young lady. I fear she has great aspirations. I shall say no more.'

Marcus had to be satisfied with this but then it came to his mind what he and his uncle had discussed. 'There is one further question I have.'

Sir Rees smiled. 'I suspected there was. Come on, ask away.'

'I was talking with my uncle the other night; he's my father's brother. The Prime Minister,' he clarified.

'I do know of him,' Sir Rees afforded a small chuckle.

'I was discussing the IDM with my uncle and we touched upon various aspects. He was quite interested actually.'

'I suspect his concern was with your involvement,' Sir Rees interjected.

'Naturally,' Marcus concurred. 'But he did raise a query that had not occurred to me and I have been giving it some thought since.'

Sir Rees interlocked his fingers and smiled. 'Not something serious, I hope. Serious enough to make you think again about making the speech?'

Marcus smiled. 'Oh no; it is nothing like that. He just asked; if the House of Commons did become free of the party system and was truly independent, what would happen to the House of Lords?'

Sir Rees unlocked his fingers and gently waved his hands. 'Ah, now that is interesting. To be honest, I am surprised the Media chaps haven't cottoned on to that earlier. It will be a matter for debate but personally, I would like it to be replaced with an elected House.'

'And independent of the party system?' Marcus asked.

'Of course,' Sir Rees replied. 'We could not have an imbalance between the Houses.'

Marcus smiled; it answered his question and made him feel better.

When Marcus left, he had a lot on his mind but most important was Sir Rees Lipton liked his speech. He needed to hone a few sentences, perhaps select some finer words but at the heart it was good. Diana was another thing entirely and he made his mind up that their relationship would in future be cordial but certainly not so close.

At around the same time that Marcus was seeing Sir Rees Lipton, James Wilder called to see Diana at her apartment. She had not been expecting him and was openly annoyed he had not rung her first.

'James, what brings you here and without a call first?' She stood in the doorway to block his entrance into her apartment but he pushed passed her.

Wilder noted her voice was somewhat cold but he was not to be put off by this young woman; she was exceptionally beautiful, he admitted but he only had thoughts that he would like to get her into his bed and nothing more. He felt that one of his major attributes was his thick skin that words never penetrated. 'I'm fed up with trying to call you. What is it with you; I forget how many times I've rung; are you deliberately avoiding speaking with me?'

Diana side-stepped his verbal onslaught; 'If you left a message to say what you wanted I may have called you back.'

'Oh yes, you want me to say I need to speak with Dolan, on the phone. You know there are ears everywhere.'

'Okay, so what do you want to speak with him about?'

'I need to speak with him,' he emphasised, 'its money matters. He's overloading the system.'

Diana roughly knew what the dealings between Dolan and Wilder were but not the detail. It was an area she wanted to keep clear of but Dolan's insistence that Wilder could only contact him through Diana was proving a pain.

'I shall give him a call for you. I think he is considering coming over again in a week or two. I'll make sure you see him.'

Wilder paused, a face to face meeting is what he badly needed but another two weeks; he breathed deeply and then nodded. 'Alright, but when you speak to him, tell him to stop feeding; he'll know what I mean.'

Diana smarted; while she did not want to know, it still rankled that she was not in the loop. 'I'll tell him. Now, is there anything else?'

Wilder looked at her for a moment; she hated it when his eyes narrowed; he looked more like the snake he was. At last he asked: 'Am I right that it was you who leaked to the Press about the PM's son making a speech at the conference?'

'Why do you assume that? I had Sir Rees making the same insinuation.'

'There were only three of us who knew; now I did not leak it, Sir Rees is too much of a gentleman to leak it and by the process of simple elimination; that only leaves one.'

Diana's face turned a high tone of red, 'Fuck you! Why would I leak it? I know I did not and I also know Sir Rees would not, so that leaves you. Why not you, answer me that you shit?'

Wilder did not lose his temper but instead, laughed loudly. 'My, what a dirty tongue you have when roused. Did you use your dirty tongue on that boy, Marcus? Is that how you....?'

But his words were abruptly ended as Diana launched herself at him; her arms were swinging but he continued to laugh as he retreated towards the door. He reached behind him and opened the door but then paused and put up his arms to ward off her attack. Diana stood motionless, breathing heavily, glaring at the man she hated.

He wanted a last jibe. 'You know, I'd love to put my cock in you and shag some sense into you.'

Diana's face flushed at the mere thought. 'I've heard that your cock is so small I wouldn't notice.'

This stung him but his voice was still full of laughter as he said, 'Don't forget to call Dolan,' and then he was gone.

Diana stood breathing heavily by the door. She had never hated a man as much as she felt hatred for Wilder at that moment. Damned if she would ring Dolan; Wilder could stew in his own juice of filth for all she cared.

She wandered over to a table and poured herself a vodka and tonic and then settled on the sofa and sipped the drink. Perhaps she had been foolish and acted too quickly but at the time she was pleased with the reaction from the media. At least it secured Marcus making the speech; he couldn't back out now, he would lose face with his father. The more she thought about it, the more confident she felt she had been right, even if it had caused a rift between her and Marcus but she was sure she could lure him back.

* * *

Matheson had received a call from the PM to meet him at the usual place but before meeting him, Sam had called and said he needed an urgent meeting with him. Matheson drove south of the river to Sam's place where Sam showed him straight into his small front room without offering a visit to the 'village' or refreshments.

Matheson noted that Sam's eyes were bright and his face showed an almost childish eagerness to impart some important information. When they were seated, Sam's began; 'I, or rather the team, have made some breakthroughs. Firstly, let me tell you about Peter Dolan or Petre Dolanski as we now know him. Simmons has done some great work. He's uncovered a network so sophisticated that the spider in the middle of the web, namely Dolan, is virtually invisible. But Simmons spotted him lurking in the dark.'

Matheson felt Sam was colouring his tale but he indulged him, knowing from experience that Sam would soon reveal the detail.

'I shall avoid the technical detail, but I have it in a full report which you can take with you and read later.'

Matheson nodded; more bed time reading.

'Right; Dolan has many fingers in many pies stretching through South and Central America mainly with drugs and he is using European outlets to launder the money. Not, you will notice when you read the report, the usual markets. He's very cunning and clever; even I have to admit that. One outlet is James Wilder the Treasurer for the IDM. Not big amounts but enough to appear to be funds for the organisation. At this point I should say, Wilder is the only one involved. This raises the question; why would Dolan get involved with a newly formed political Movement? I had a meeting with Simmons and Roberts; Simmons is expert on IT matters but

Roberts is quite fluent with matters financial. Our considered opinion is, if the IDM get into a position of power and Wilder is the Chancellor, it will be an open channel for Dolan to filter his money in, not only through government loans and projects, but also investing in the City.'

Sam paused; if possible, his eyes were even brighter. He waited for Matheson to comment but he merely nodded to indicate he was following Sam's reasoning.

'Now; I know I said Wilder was the only one involved, but that is the financial side. There is another person.' Sam paused again; perhaps just for the dramatic effect he knew it would have; 'Dolan is married to Diana Bright, or should I say, Mrs. Diana Dolanski. They secretly married in Buenos Aires about two years ago.'

Matheson sat up, 'Now that answers several questions.'

'Indeed,' Sam smiled; 'I believe that young lady deliberately seduced young Marcus into the Movement and to making a speech at their conference in a months' time. We do not have any direct evidence that she is directly involved with the financial matters but she will definitely be a conduit between Dolan and Wilder.'

Matheson stood up, there was not much room to walk about but he needed to think and what better way than to step around the small room, threading his way between furniture. At last he stopped and looked down at Sam; 'Where is Dolan at this moment?'

'I have been expecting him to make a visit here; I assume he will need to see his many business contacts, but at the moment he remains in Buenos Aires.'

'Alright, tell Simmons to keep beavering away and find out any more strands to Dolan's web and Wilder's involvement. This may be the time I should speak with our friends across the pond. I want you to get closer to Marcus; I have a feeling he may need our help before this is through.'

He looked down at Sam who nodded he understood.

'And I think,' Matheson added, 'we ought to get Marcus away for a while; somewhere safe and under our control. Can you talk to him?'

'Of course,' Sam replied.

Matheson picked up his copy of the report. 'I have to go to see the PM. At his insistence,' he added.

Matheson parked his car in the usual place and waited. The air was still and colouring blue; that half-light between early evening and night. He was annoyed the PM had requested the meeting, mainly because he knew the PM was still smarting from the fact his son was going to go ahead and make the speech and how well the news of it had been grabbed by the media. He suspected the PM would insist something had to be done. His thoughts were broken when he saw the PM's black Jaguar pull in behind him. Matheson switched on the recorder.

The PM slumped heavily into the passenger seat and again offered no greeting.

'Have you made any progress? Have you anything to tell me?'

Matheson edged towards his door so that their shoulders were not touching; he disliked any thought of contact with this man. 'It was you who called this meeting. I would have called you if there was anything, Prime Minister. I really think we should keep these meetings to a minimum.'

The PM twisted in his seat. 'Oh you do, do you? Well, I decide when we should meet and I wanted to see you now.' He seemed lost for words for a minute before gathering himself for his next outburst. 'You have no idea what damage my son has caused me.' Matheson leaned away as the PM's mouth was intrusively too near his ear. 'I am beset from all sides, especially from the media and I need; no, I demand some action. It is going to be even worse when he makes that damn speech. Now, what can you tell me?'

Matheson became determined not to tell him about Dolan; the PM would probably demand immediate action and Matheson was not ready for that yet; not until Sam had finished his research on him. 'We have made some good progress but we need documentary evidence. We are in the process of gathering that right now.'

The PM sighed heavily. 'You mean there is something rotten in the IDM. I knew it.' He paused while he chewed this over. 'Alright, I'll leave it with you but I want some results and soon. It will be the conference season in September and I would like a few heads to display on the end of pikes,' he laughed at his attempted, instant humour. 'I have also decided that you should deal directly with the Home Secretary, Toby Fennel. He'll be contacting you. He has closer contact with the security forces. I am hoping they will be needed when you round them all up.' Then he leaned closely, 'And I want my son to be one of them.'

Matheson was stilled in shock but the PM was already getting out of the car before he could question him. He reached forward and switched off the recorder. He waited until the PM's car had driven off before starting his car and heading for the home of his Head of Department. Although he had been told he was not to contact him unless it was a very serious circumstance, he wanted to appraise him with the developing situation and ask advice, no matter how obscure his Head may keep it.

Matheson pulled up in a road flanked by very large Victorian style houses and looked across at one which showed lights on the ground floor. He rang a number from his mobile, a special restricted number and waited. A voice answered in a mono syllable.

He decided not to offer an excuse for the call but get right into the heart of the matter; he did not want the Head to easily dismiss him. 'I need to see you right away, sir; a bit of an emergency has come up.'

There was the slightest pause before the Head responded. 'I shall have to see when...'

'I am outside; across the road from your house,' Matheson said to pre-empt him putting him off. Matheson thought he heard a quiet curse.

'Then you had better come over.' The call ended.

Edward Staniforth, the Head of the Section met Matheson at the front door and showed him into a side room. He felt he wanted to remind Matheson of the laid down protocol but he knew Matheson well enough to guess his presence was due to an emergency situation; or it had better be.

Staniforth indicated towards a chair and sat in one facing it; he offered no refreshment and spoke in a direct voice. 'So what is the emergency?'

He listened without interruption as Matheson told him all he knew and with special emphasis on the PM's insistence that his son be included with any who were taken into custody.

'The point is, sir, apart from what we suspect about Dolan and Wilder and the fact that Diana Bright is really married to Dolan, we have not found anything else remotely subversive about the Movement's activities and certainly not with Sir Rees Lipton and especially not with the PM's son.'

'This Dolanski or Dolan, must have other contacts outside the Movement; have you made any progress there?' the Head asked.

'We are following that through and I am thinking of going across the Pond to see my counterpart in the CIA. I'm sure Dolanski's business stretches into the US. But tonight, the PM told me he was handing everything over to the Home Secretary. To me that means he is distancing himself when he expects us to arrest his son.'

Staniforth tutted loudly, 'The Home Secretary will be like a bull dog. He's a man with high ambition and little intelligence; I have clashed with him in the past. I think you are right to have brought me up to date.' He thought for a moment. 'You say you do not suspect there are others involved in the Movement. It is probably a small, tight knit group around this Dolanski. Concentrate on him and Wilder and any associates.'

He paused and then added, 'Of course, finding out that this Diana woman is Dolanski's wife also opens more possibilities.' Staniforth thought for a moment. 'Whatever happens, we must not allow the Home Secretary to unleash the security forces. You have contacts in MI6 and MI5; have a chat with them and apprise them of the situation and see if they have anything. And you had better warn them about Fennel taking over. That'll shake them up.'

Matheson was encouraged by Staniforth's response. 'The PM said he would tell the Home Secretary to contact me to bring him up to date. I hope I can convince him we should play it low key.'

'It depends upon how the PM positions it with him. He well knows the Home Secretary is like a Pitbull and he's deliberately hoping he will charge in with head down and jaws gnashing. Open our usual channel again and keep me informed of everything.' Staniforth inclined his head in question and Matheson nodded.

'I shall do that sir, and thank you for your support.'

Staniforth then surprised him when he finally said, 'This is heading for one God Almighty mess and I do not intend us to be smeared with Fennel's ambitions. Be wary of him. He may appear an idiot but he is a dangerous idiot.'

Matheson felt a little better when he left and drove immediately across the river; he needed another long talk with Sam.

He arrived again outside the small, terraced house;

he had rung ahead and Sam would be expecting him. Their greeting was brief and Sam showed Matheson straight into the front room and when they were seated asked, 'So how did Staniforth take you breaking the protocol?'

Matheson allowed himself a thin smile, 'I think he was prepared to chew me over but at least he gave me the chance to explain my visit and when he had heard what I had to say, he was surprisingly supportive. He was very supportive, in fact. Staniforth may have his little eccentricities but he is straight when it comes to the security of the realm. He has warned me about Fennel. I thought we were having a difficult time with the PM but Fennel is something else.'

'Has Fennel contacted you yet?' Sam asked.

'No, the PM won't have had time yet to brief him but when he does, I expect Fennel to call a meeting of the heads of all the security forces and the Met. I intend to contact my friends in MI5 and MI6 and appraise them with the situation before Fennel calls a meeting.'

Sam smiled. 'You do realise you are sticking your neck out.'

'And Fennel and the PM will fight over who chops it off.' Matheson smiled. 'You know Sam, I don't really care. I have decided this will be my last action before I retire.'

'You have told me that before but make sure you

retire with a pension and not a prison sentence.'

'Oh, I think I am covering the proverbial backside. That is why I saw Staniforth; I need him on my side and when I have spoken with the various intelligence areas, I feel confident even the PM will say nothing. I do have certain recordings just for back-up.'

Sam shook his head. 'I didn't expect things to get this dirty when we started this project but I suppose that is what politics have become these days.'

'Not politics in general,' Matheson argued, 'it's more to do with the individuals involved. Well, certain people.'

'So, what are our next steps?' Sam enquired.

'You know what you and Simmons and Roberts have to do and it has become urgent that you find out as much as you can as quickly as you can. When Fennel gets involved, I expect he'll come charging out like a bull with its tail on fire. Oh, and what I said about young Marcus, I think it is imperative that he is secreted away before anyone can get at him.'

Sam nodded, 'I have already thought of speaking with him. He may be a little bit awkward about it but I can persuade him.'

Matheson stood and sighed. Sam watched him closely; he had known Matheson for more years than he cared remember; he was good, the best but now he was looking older and Sam was concerned his boss, his friend, had that certain darkness around his eyes that showed weariness from doing something he did not believe in.

'We have had hard cases over the years, Sam, but this one is dirty and involves a Prime Minister and more important, his son. I do not want the boy destroyed from all this.'

His maternal comment surprised Sam. 'Don't worry,' he assured Matheson, 'I shall look out for him.'

CHAPTER SIX
THE CALM BEFORE THE STORM

Matheson took a taxi cab from his office to Sir Rees Lipton's town house; the traffic too heavy and the distance too short for him to drive in his own car. He had rung Sir Rees the night before and arranged the meeting for eleven-o-clock that morning. He was shown in to Sir Rees's working office and Sir Rees rose from his chair and came round his desk with his hand extended.

'John, it was a surprise when you called last night but a pleasant one, I have to quickly add. How are you?'

Matheson took his hand and shook it warmly. 'It was good to hear your voice again and I was pleased you still remembered me.'

Sir Rees tutted and ushered Matheson to a chair and then, instead of sitting behind his desk, he pulled over a chair and sat facing to him. 'You have aged well; you look so fit and healthy. You'll have to tell me the secret before you leave.'

'No secret. Avoid nothing but keep it in moderation. Stress is as damaging as a wrong diet.'

Sir Rees chuckled and at that moment, the door

opened and the butler pushed a small metal trolley in and positioned it between the seats before leaving without a word. 'Thank you, Jameson,' Sir Rees said before Jameson disappeared.

'I ordered coffee for you. I think you will enjoy this. This is Jamaica Blue Mountain. Not a lot available at the moment; they had a bad harvest.' He poured two cups and relaxed back. 'Don't add milk if you like the taste of coffee. I think you will appreciate the soft flavour.'

Matheson sipped, paused and then sipped again. 'My, that is a good coffee. Where do you get it; I shall have to buy some.'

'As I said, it is in short supply but I shall provide you with a few pounds of beans. Keep it refrigerated and only grind the beans as you use them.' He sipped his own coffee and sat back and allowed his hands to hang limp over the arms of the chair. 'Now, tell me, what have you been doing since you left university? I spoke with Ralph last night and told him I was seeing you and he said it was about time the two of you met up again and had a few beers.'

'It has been too many years since last I saw him,' Matheson mused. 'Please let me have his 'phone number.'

'I shall, so, what have you been up to? I think you are something to do with the Security Force.'

Matheson smiled and carefully selected his words.

'Yes, something akin to that but I keep very much in the backroom. I am concerned with security in the country but that can take many forms.'

Sir Rees lowered his brow slightly and looked at him with hooded eyes. 'Am I a security risk? Is that what brings you here?'

Matheson put down his cup. 'No, emphatically not, please let me try to explain. The IDM is a comparatively new movement but you are making incredible advances at local and national levels. I am making just a routine visit to speak with you, in confidence I assure you, to assess your opinion on your movement.'

'Why?' Sir Rees persisted, but Matheson cut in.

'It is routine, I assure you. We keep a watching brief on many organisations, political and otherwise. It is just part of ensuring the realm is at peace and not threatened.' Matheson smiled broadly to assuage Sir Rees's obvious suspicion. 'Through the past few years, your Movement has made spectacular gains with the public and in local and national government. It is only natural that we keep.... er... shall we say, a quiet observation on the activities.'

'And have you found anything untoward?'

Matheson lifted his cup but it was empty. 'May I have some more of your superb coffee?'

Sir Rees lifted the coffee pot and refilled his cup but he suspected Matheson was stalling a little and perhaps had some bad news to impart. 'Well?' His voice was a little strained.

Matheson sipped the coffee and gently replaced the cup. 'It is really a very small matter. A case of a few loose ends, nothing more.'

'Then please tell me what they are,' Sir Rees's voice was a little taut.

'Diana Bright has come to our attention.'

Sir Rees smiled broadly as if with some relief. 'Ah, now that young lady, well I am sure you are well aware of her position as Head of Administration and Relations but,' he tilted his head to one side and pointed a finger at Matheson. 'You are concerned with her relationship with young Marcus McVey.'

Matheson nodded, he was pleased Sir Rees had raised that subject; it may open an opportunity to ask what he really wanted to know. 'Of course, he is a high profile person and we have to keep a guard on anything to do with the Prime Minister.'

Sir Rees relaxed and allowed himself a chuckle. 'I don't think you have any worries there. As you are probably aware, she is a remarkably attractive young lady and single and when they were introduced, young Marcus was immediately smitten by her. Quite frankly, I see nothing wrong from their relationship.'

Matheson noted the word 'single' so Sir Rees was not aware of her marriage to Dolan. 'And you have full confidence in her?'

Sir Rees pressed his hands together. 'She is a very knowledgeable and industrious girl. She studied at Oxford and Yale and gained honours at both. We were lucky to get her on board. Her only problem is her looks. She uses them to get the best from her colleagues but at the same time, inadvertently smites their hearts.'

'What about Wilder?'

Sir Rees's face darkened for a moment. 'What about him?'

'I have heard that he does not get on with Diana Bright.'

Sir Rees relaxed. 'Oh, I see, well he is a very strong character and just between you and me, he fancies himself as a ladies' man but Diana can't stand him. I don't know if he once over stepped the mark, she has not said, but to be honest, I would not be surprised. He is very good as the Financial Secretary for the Movement but I have had a quiet word with him to tone down his language in mixed company and shall we say, his overt gestures with some of the younger female staff.'

'Does he control all the finances for the Movement?' Matheson asked.

'Pretty well; as I said he is very good at his job and of course we have our own internal Auditors. As far as I am concerned, everything is above board. Is there a problem?'

Matheson shook his head; it was obvious to him that Sir Rees was not aware of what he and his team had discovered. He thought he would try one more probe. 'Have you ever heard of the name Dolan?'

Sir Rees tilted his head to one side and thought for a moment. 'No. I'm sure I have not. Should I have?'

Matheson decided that it was time for him to end the meeting before Sir Rees started asking his own probing questions. 'No, it is just a name we have come across and probably has no connection to your movement. Well, I must thank you for your time, Sir Rees,' Matheson stood and held out his hand.

Sir Rees stood and shook his hand warmly. 'It has been a pleasure. Don't forget to get in touch with Ralph; I suspect the two of you will sink a few beers over your reminiscing.'

As he was leaving, Sir Rees handed him a small parcel. 'Some Jamaica Blue, it should last a while and give you time to find more.'

After Matheson had left, Sir Rees pondered over their conversation and wondered if it had been as social as Matheson had made out. He decided when he visited the Movement's centre next; he would make enquiries about the name 'Dolan'.

The next day as Sir Rees was taking the lift up to his office; Wilder entered on the second floor and pressed the button for the fifth floor. They exchanged pleasantries and then fell silent for a while. When the lift stopped at the fifth floor and the doors opened, Wilder nodded and made to leave.

'Just a quick question,' Sir Rees said. 'Have you heard of the name Dolan? Within our organisation, that is?'

Wilder shook his head. 'No.' He stepped out.

After the lift doors had closed, Wilder stood for a moment. He felt an empty sensation stir inside. Dolan; where would Sir Rees have heard that name? He wondered who could be the source. He stood, slowly shaking his head; he was very troubled. Only he and Diana knew about Dolan and no way would she have mentioned him; she would have no reason to. Someone came out of an office down the corridor to shake him from his thoughts. He made his way to his office.

He sat in his chair behind his large, mahogany desk and rested his elbows upon the desk top and his chin upon his hands. He sighed. He hated questions when he did not have an answer. The names Dolan and Sir Rees circled in his mind. He could not go back to Sir Rees and ask him where he heard of the name 'Dolan'. Could he?

* * *

Sam was in his small office at the Movement's Headquarters but had been keeping an eye for Marcus. Just before lunchtime, after making several futile calls to Marcus's mobile, he had finally caught him and asked him to meet him in the Headquarters. He looked up from his desk as Marcus entered his room.

Sam leapt to his feet. 'Marcus!' he said, 'I'm so glad you could come.'

'Hello Sam, what did you want me for?'

Sam motioned with his hand for Marcus to sit down and he closed the door when Marcus had entered. 'I have been wanting a word with you,' Sam said and indicated for Marcus to sit in the chair next to his desk. 'I wanted to ask you about the Press. Have they been bothering you?'

Marcus laughed. 'Have they, I know now the real meaning of cat and mouse games. The only time I can get in and out of my apartment is in the small hours using the rear entrance. Don't they ever give up?'

'I'm afraid not, not from my experience. I wanted to suggest I have a country house near Arundel left to me by some dotty old aunt when she died and if you wanted some peace then I am quite happy for you to use it. I can drive you down there so they don't recognise and follow your car.'

Marcus reached across the desk and touched Sam's

arm. 'That is good of you but I have arranged to stay at my uncle's place for a while or at least until the conference. I hope after making the speech that they will leave me alone.'

'Your uncle, now would that be your father's brother? I wouldn't advise you go there. The Press will be aware of him and have probably already got a stakeout arranged there.'

Marcus thought for a moment. 'I would be grateful if you could drive me there in your car? That could throw them off the scent.'

Sam rubbed his hand across his chin. 'It may for a while but I think staying at my place would be better. It would guarantee they wouldn't know where you were.'

'You are probably right, Sam, but it is still a few weeks to the conference and I'm going to go scatty on my own dodging the Press. I have just about finished the speech. It just needs a bit of polish and I know the person to help. I also have a special project for my work which I should be giving more of my time to.'

'Well then, this place I have will be ideal and if you need to have your things, you know, your architect tools, I can arrange to have them moved as well.'

Marcus smiled but hesitated, 'Is there a particular reason you want me out of the way, Sam?'

It was Sam's turn to hesitate. 'Look, can we meet tonight for a drink. I would like to have a chat with you.' He saw Marcus's expression change. 'It's nothing to worry about but I should explain a few things to you. This speech you are going to make is causing a few waves in certain quarters and I think I should give you some advice on how to handle it.'

Marcus nodded. 'I think you understand the position I am in.'

More than you know, thought Sam but said, 'Good, so tonight, I can pick you up at eight?'

Marcus nodded and then smiled and Sam relaxed.

Around six-o-clock that evening, Marcus was in his apartment packing his case when his intercom buzzed. He lifted the receiver and viewed the small screen which showed the entrance hall to the building; it was Diana.

'What brings you round here?' he asked.

Diana looked up, directly to the camera. 'I just wanted a talk with you. Just a brief chat, I promise.'

Marcus sighed but pressed the button to allow her to enter. He opened the door to his apartment and waited for the lift to rise to his floor. The door slid back and Diana, flustered with her flame hair flowing back, quickly crossed and entered his apartment without a word. He followed her in and closed the door.

'No Press men about?' he queried.

She shook her head, 'I have had them following me about too. They keep shouting about you making your speech, asking if I know what you will be saying.' She stepped closer to him and put both hands on his shoulders. 'Oh, Marcus, I am sorry you are being put through all this. I think it must have been Wilder who tipped them off. God, I do hate that man!'

Marcus tried to pull away from her but she clung tight and proffered her lips to his mouth. He tilted his head away. 'Diana, we need to talk. I am going away until the Conference.'

She looked startled. 'Oh, where are you going to? Can I come with you?'

'You can't,' he said quickly. 'You have too much work for the conference and I need some time alone. Besides, I have this special project for my firm and I must concentrate to get that finished.'

Her hands slipped from his shoulders and her face formed a pained expression. 'And alone from me, I suppose. I've noticed you seem to be cooling off towards me. Have I done something wrong to upset you?'

His brain said, tell her the truth but his words came out differently. 'Since the leak about my making the speech, I have been hounded by the Press; my boss has side lined me away from the office and my fiancé has ended our relationship.' He knew he should also have mentioned his suspicions about her but he saw her bite on her lower lip and her green eyes seemed to shade darker with sadness. 'Diana...'

She cut off his words by suddenly moving forward and crushing her body against him and before he could react, she kissed him hard upon his lips. He felt the very breathe leave his body and his arms went around her.

'Darling,' she whispered at last, 'make love to me. I want you...'

But he stilled her words as he kissed her and together, in some dance macabre, they edged into the bedroom, casting their clothing as they went.

The same mist had enveloped him as it always did when they made love; the world seemed to disappear with all its worries and tribulations and he floated with her to another level; a cocoon in the ether where they were only conscious of each other's bodies; softness and warmth with no time. Time!

Marcus sat up and looked at his watch. It was seven-thirty and Sam would be calling for him in thirty minutes. His sudden movement had awoken Diana and she slid a lazy arm across his chest but he rolled away and stood up.

'I am sorry,' he uttered, 'I have someone calling for me at eight. I have to go with him. Please, you must leave now!'

Diana propped herself on one arm. 'Now that is a new way to dismiss a young maiden after taking advantage of her.' She giggled.

Marcus looked around for his clothes on the floor. 'I am serious, Diana. This man is very important and he mustn't know you are here.'

She pouted, 'And who is this very important person who drags away my Prince Valiant? Forsooth, am I just a harlot who you dismiss after taking her maidenhood?'

Even Marcus had to laugh at her description of herself as he hopped from one leg to the other as he put on his boxer shorts. 'Enough of that my young maiden; believe me, this man must not know you are here and certainly not in my bed.'

Diana sat up, her delicious breasts causing him to look at her with longing. Again, her face took on a hurt expression. 'And just who is this person and why are you going with him and where to?'

Marcus pulled on his shirt and then his trousers and sat on the bed again to pull on his socks. She put her hands on his shoulders to distract him.

Marcus tried to shrug her away. 'Who he is and where we are going does not concern you. The fact is; I need some me time to get this speech finished and to get on with my work. I am an architect you know and my boss has been good enough to give me a special project where I can work alone and get away from this... this maelstrom of attention from the media guys.'

Diana let her hands fall. 'Oh, alright, I see you

don't trust me.' She swung off the bed and began collecting her own clothes.

Marcus stood up and slipped his feet into his shoes. 'It is not a question of trust, it is what I have just said and only that,' he lied.

Somehow he managed to get her to dress and ushered, with continuing protests, out of the door and he watched her until the lift door slid shut. He hurried back into his apartment and finished his packing. He stood upright, sighed and looked at his watch. It was a minute to eight and as if on cue, the buzzer sounded.

Outside, Diana had walked a short distance from the front door and then stepped into a doorway and stood watching. A small figure came down the street, paused at the door and pressed the buzzer. For Diana, it answered one question but posed another. She recognised Sam but why was he calling on Marcus at this time? She waited until the figure had entered the building and then she traced her steps to her car.

Marcus ushered Sam into the lounge and indicated an armchair for him to sit. 'Can I get you a drink?' he asked, 'I can only offer coffee or tea.' But Sam shook his head.

'We can go out if you want a beer or something stronger,' Sam said, 'but first I would like a talk with you.'

Marcus stood for a moment but when Sam did

not continue, he sat in another chair and clasped his hands together. 'Sam, I have been pondering about what you said earlier today. Would I be right in assuming you are more than just an administrator at the IDM?'

Sam nodded. 'I thought you might ponder on that. I will be open and honest with you; you deserve that much. I work for the Security Service.' He paused but Marcus said nothing, his face displayed nothing. 'I was placed there to, shall we say, to look around, to make sure everything was, well, everything was above board.' Marcus was about to say something but Sam held up his hand. 'It is quite normal. It is a new movement, politics and all that. We keep a watching brief on all political activities, including, I might add, the current MP's and party activities. Defence of the realm and all that.'

'And I come in your remit? I suppose I would,' Marcus answered his own question. 'Being who I am and how I am now involved.'

'Quite,' Sam agreed.

'Can I ask, has my father requested you to look after me?'

Sam so wanted to tell him the truth but he held back. 'You sort of thrust yourself into our sphere, so to speak.'

'And the reason to seclude me away for a few weeks,' Marcus asked, 'whose idea is that?'

'Mine, actually,' Sam answered. 'Apart from the Media interest, there may be some who would prefer you not to make your speech.'

Marcus chewed this over for a moment. 'Do you mean; to physically try to stop me?'

Sam flapped his hands and tried to chuckle it away. 'Not that drastic. Just prevent you from making the speech. Now,' he hastened on, hoping to end that line of questions, 'I have talked with my superior and he agrees that you should go somewhere that ensures your location is unknown until the time for the Conference. As I said, we have a safe location where all mod-cons are provided and you, as you said, can get on with your work.'

Marcus lowered his head and sat for long minutes thinking this over. Finally he raised his head, 'Alright, but I must insist that I spend this weekend with my uncle. He is my closest friend right now and not, I should add, a friend of my father; quite the reverse in fact.'

Sam knew all about the relationship between the two brothers and nodded his assent. 'So, I shall drive you tonight in my car to your Uncle Robert's place; near Gloucester I believe, and then I shall call for you at noon on Monday and drive you to our safe location.'

Marcus hesitated. 'What about my drawing instruments? I have to work on this project.'

'Do you have them here in your apartment?' asked Sam.

'Yes, I have a spare set of everything I need here. I often work from home.'

'Then fine; gather it all together and give me a spare key and I will arrange for my men to collect them over the weekend and deliver them to the safe location.'

Marcus laughed. 'It includes my drawing board. That's quite a size.'

Sam shook his head. 'No problem, just make sure it is all in one place and we shall take care of it.'

Marcus stood up and looked down on the smaller figure. 'You know, Sam, I am putting a lot of trust in you.'

'I'm glad you think you can.'

Marcus's face became serious. 'Don't let me down. What I am doing is important; very important.'

Sam stood also, 'I know and you have my full support. Follow me and you will come to no harm.' Sam reached forward and touched the young man's arm. 'Never lose faith in me.'

Marcus nodded and then added, 'I did as you suggested. I have a new phone and I have notified only those people I want to talk with.'

'Yes, I saw your new number come up on my phone. Now, let's get your bags packed and we should head west.'

Matheson had a busy day, first contacting people

he knew in MI5 and MI6 and arranging to see them. At each meeting with representatives whom he knew personally, which helped his cause, he candidly explained what was going on and ended each meeting with a warning about the Home Secretary and what he was about to ask or rather, demand they do. He gained verbal assurances they would work together with him and discuss with him when the Home Secretary contacted them.

That evening, he received a phone call from the Home Secretary to meet him in his office immediately. Matheson had been expecting the call but not so immediate. He went, feeling somewhat uneasily to the Home office.

'I'm glad you came here so promptly,' Fennel said, without getting up from his seat. He waved his hand to indicate a seat in front of his desk. Matheson sat and noticed was that Fennel's seat was adjustable and he had it cranked up high so that he looked down on whoever was on the other side of the desk. This made him smile inwardly; the little runt felt at a physical advantage.

'The PM has told you that I am to take over the IDM case and as of now, you will report directly to me and not to him.'

This short statement confirmed two things to Matheson. Firstly, the PM was taking a deliberate backward step and putting Fennel's arse on the line and the mention of the word case meant Fennel saw it as legal activity which it certainly was not. In addition, to Matheson's delight, he could tell from Fennel's smiling demeanour, that the little shit saw himself as a pseudo Prime Minister; this meant his mind would be elevating him to a superior level and his ego would blind his mind to detail and sense.

In its place would be suspicion and a sort of paranoia that, while it could make him dangerous, it also meant he would react to any suggestion and Matheson had plenty he could suggest that would keep Fennel chasing his tail.

Fennel waited for Matheson to respond but receiving nothing, he continued, mistakenly thinking that Matheson was somehow in awe of his presence. 'The PM has brought me up to date with the details of this case and I must say I am disappointed. I assume you have taken all this upon yourself, for whatever reason, and your effort has not shown much of a result.'

Matheson felt even more relaxed. So, he thought, you are not aware of the team I have put together and you have not spoken with Staniforth. At last he felt he ought to say something. 'I will be honest with you,' which of course he was not, 'I have put in a lot of work on this case as you put it, and there is little wrong within the IDM structure.'

'That is what you think,' Fennel's voice carried an

edge of sarcasm, 'well I disagree.'

'Based on what?' Matheson interrupted.

Fennel did not like the interruption and he eased himself back in his chair and crossed his hands over his lap. 'I'll tell you what, I have it on good authority that there are dark dealings going on at the highest level and I shall be exposing them very soon.'

Matheson guessed rightly that Fennel was lying and he would make a lousy Poker player but he decided, for now, not to antagonise him further. 'I have been instructed by the PM to give you all my assistance and naturally, I shall do so.'

Fennel grinned; he knew he could bring this lap dog to heel. 'I shall let you know in due course. In the meantime, carry on with your...' he paused for effect, 'your enquiries. I shall be setting up meetings with MI5 and MI6. I shall be briefing them on their role.'

'You feel you need their involvement?' Matheson queried.

'Look', Fennel raised his hand and began to wag a finger like a condescending schoolmaster. 'I have had my suspicions about this IDM for quite a while. The PM has similar reservations but he is too busy at the moment, financial problems, and so he has passed the baton to me. He and I are in accord. There is something rotten in the state of Denmark.' Fennel smiled thinking he had made a literary quote.

Matheson almost asked if it were bacon but

decided such a comment would only confuse the proceedings. He was satisfied that Fennel knew little or next to nothing and so Matheson rose, nodded and left. He sat in his car and contacted his opposite numbers in MI5 and MI6 and passed on his meeting with Fennel. After their laughter subsided, he drove across London and met with Staniforth to brief him on his encounter with Fennel.

CHAPTER SEVEN
A TIME FOR REFLECTION

Their journey to his Uncle Robert's was uneventful and driven mainly in silence. Marcus slept some of the way and was surprised when Sam slowed the car and eased up the drive way to his uncle's house.

'You found the way alright to Mateley Hill I see?' Marcus said.

'You gave me the address and I used the Satnav on silence,' Sam replied.

There were lights on in the house and Marcus saw the front door open and his Uncle Robert stepped out onto the veranda. Sam got out and went round to the rear door, released the catch and handed Marcus his two cases.

'I will not come in with you,' Sam said, 'I'll leave you to excuse me.'

'Do you not want to meet my uncle,' Marcus asked, 'you must want a drink or something.'

'There's an all-night café, I saw a few miles back. I'll freshen up there. You go on, please.' Sam laid his hand on Marcus shoulder and gave it a squeeze. 'I'll be back at noon on Monday.' Then, without another word he got back in the car. Marcus watched him back out and then drive away. He shook his head and then turned, Robert was coming towards him.

'My boy,' he hailed. 'Your friend is a little shy?'

Marcus took his proffered hand. 'He's a busy man,' he excused.

'A security man,' Robert ventured.

'Why do you say that?' asked Marcus.

'When your father became PM they paid us a visit. Three cars came all the same as that one. SUV's or something; must be standard issue. They said they came to check our security in the house in case we became targets. Well, that was their excuse. Julia stopped them from nosing around the whole place. Come in, the girls are still up waiting to see you. Here, let me help with your cases.'

Julia met him in the hall with a big hug and a kiss and Celia, a little behind her, came forward and gave him a loose hug and with her head turned aside. She was never the one for showing that sort of emotion.

He left his cases in the hall and followed them into the lounge; it felt like he was coming home. 'I have prepared a little supper,' Celia said.

'And I prepared your bed,' Julia smiled, a certain light in her eyes. Celia coughed and left for the kitchen.

'But first, a drink,' Robert said, moving to the drinks cabinet, where he poured a large JD into a whiskey glass and then an equally large malt for himself. He passed the JD drink to Marcus and indicated he should sit. 'Well, my boy, what have you been up to that deserves a free lift from the Security Service?'

Julia had gone into the kitchen and returned with a bottle of Budweiser. 'What's this about the Security Service?' she asked.

Marcus half laughed to brush it aside. 'He's a good friend of mine. Yes, he does work in the Security Force but it was just a favour.'

'Is your car broken down?' asked Robert.

Marcus realised his mistake and sipped his bourbon. 'Actually, it is a little more complicated but Sam, that's the chap who drove me here, has become a close friend and when I told him I was coming here to see you, he suggested he should drive me in his car and avoid any media people following me.'

'Oh, they've been here already,' Julia said. 'Even tried to get in the house but I saw them off.'

Robert laughed. 'You should have seen them run when Julia chased them with a garden rake.'

'I'm sorry,' Marcus apologised, 'I feel that this is my fault.'

'Nonsense,' Robert said, 'It was the person who leaked the fact that you were going to make a speech who has caused all this. You stick at it and bollocks to the lot of them.'

'Father!' Celia cried as she entered the room with a tray of sandwiches and an assortment of heated nibbles. She placed it on a small side table. 'There, that should fill empty spaces. I see you have arranged the drinks, father. I was going to make tea or Ovaltine.'

'Go and have your cocoa, Ces, and don't mind the grown-ups,' Julia laughed.

Celia returned to the kitchen without a word but did exude a loud sniff to show her disapproval.

Robert got up and went over to the tray of food. 'Now Julia, it's too late at night to be goading your sister. Here, Marcus, tuck in, she's provided a good spread.' He looked pointedly at Julia and spoke through a mouthful of sandwich, 'At least your sister knows how to do the useful things in this house.'

Julia lifted a baked prawn and dipped it in a sauce. 'I didn't see her chasing away those chaps with a rake.'

'No,' Robert laughed softly, 'I suppose you've got your uses.'

Marcus joined them at the table and the three of them munched their way through the food. 'Sam,' Marcus said at last, 'that's the chap who drove me here, will be picking me up at noon on Monday.'

Julia made a noise like a cat mewing. 'I thought you were staying here for a couple of weeks.'

'I'm sorry, that was the plan but Sam, and his boss, thought it best if I stay at a place where the media don't know; just for some peace.'

'More like a safe house,' Robert conjectured, he

looked pointedly at Marcus.

Marcus looked down and selected another sandwich. 'I suppose it is something like that but the longer I am here, the more likely the media bods will cotton on and then you will all be involved.'

Robert coughed and spoke in a soft but serious tone. 'Marcus, are you in some sort of trouble? Is there some sort of threat against you?'

Marcus felt his face redden slightly. 'Who would want to threaten me?'

Robert took up his glass and refilled it with his favourite malt whiskey. 'I can think of one person.'

'Your brother, Uncle John,' Julia said quickly.

Robert nodded. 'I wouldn't put anything passed him.' He looked again at Marcus and raised his eyebrows with a question.

Marcus tried to shrug it away but was not convincing. 'They are arranging for all my design kit to be taken to this secret place. I shall be able to get on with this special project I have, in some peace.'

Robert whirled his glass around and studied the pale liquid. He looked up, 'It is very late. I think we should go to our beds and we can talk in the morning.'

'That was the purpose I have come here,' Marcus said. 'I wanted to discuss a few things and get your advice.'

'And our advice you shall get,' Robert said, 'and

now off you go young man and try to relax. You're in good company here.'

'I'll come with you,' Julia said with a sideways glance to Marcus. 'We've put you in another room at the end of the house. 'It will be... ' she was about to say safer but quickly changed it to say, 'it will be quieter.'

Marcus carried the larger case and Julia the smaller one, up to his room. It was a large bedroom, well furnished with plenty of cupboard space and an en suite shower room and it was situated at the end of the upper hallway which traversed the house.

'I think you will be cosy here,' Julia said, 'of course, the maid service comes in various forms.'

Marcus crossed to her, kissed her lightly on the lips and then placed his hands on her shoulders and marched her slowly backwards to the door.

'Bully boots,' she said.

'Oh sweet maiden, were this another time and place how I would welcome you to my bosom,' he said as he eased her through the doorway.

'You're still a bully boots,' she reached up quickly and kissed him. 'You don't know what you are missing.'

'I have a good imagination,' he said and closed the door.

* * *

Earlier that evening, Fennel contacted the PM and insisted on a meeting that evening. McVey reluctantly agreed in case Fennel had something important from his meeting with Matheson. They met upstairs in Number 10 in the PM's flat who was determined that when he had finished with Fennel, he would for once, get an early night. Though a large man with reserves of strength, the past few weeks were beginning to take their toll on him.

He had not been eating or sleeping well and put most of that down to his son's threat. He knew Marcus was quite able to put together a speech that would hone in on him as a father and the PM and he feared his reputation for strength in adversity may be undermined. Now, of all times, he needed to appear strong even if it meant sacrificing his son to do so.

When Fennel arrived, the PM offered no drinks and he did not offer to sit down; he wanted to keep the meeting as short as possible. He emphasised this by opening their meeting with: 'I want to keep this short, Toby as I have some important documents to go through before going to the House tomorrow.' It was a lie but lately, they were coming easily.

Fennel smiled his acceptance. 'I understand, John.'

The PM noted Fennel's use of his first name but let it pass. 'Well, what is so important?'

'I have had a meeting with that Security guy; Matheson I think is his name, he didn't impress me and didn't have a lot to impart and I have decided upon a course of action.'

Fennel paused and the PM sighed. 'So what is it you have decided that is so important to see me tonight?'

He found it difficult to hide his irritation and Fennel stumbled a little for the right words while questioning if rushing to the PM was such a good idea. He had sat for over an hour working out a strategy and at the time, it seemed to him he had solved the problem and was buoyed to explain it to the PM. Now, he was not so sure.

'I have come up with a plan that I think will strike the IDM at their most vulnerable moment.'

The PM waited and then said, 'Well, what is it?'

'Well, it is all to do with timing. Their Conference is in two weeks in Brighton and so during that time, they will be concentrating on that. I will call a meeting with MI5 and MI6 next week and set up a Special Branch task force to raid certain homes and offices of selected heads of the organisation. There are five specific ones I have identified at the moment. We can scupper their whole conference before it happens. The Press will have a field day.'

The PM looked up at the ceiling. 'My God,' he thought, 'what have I unleashed?'

'Prime Minister, what...?' Fennel saw the look on the PM's face and was confused.

The Prime Minister gathered himself. 'Look, for a

start, we do not have enough evidence against anyone or the whole bloody organisation. I certainly do not want MI5 and MI6 involved until we know for sure and exactly who. If we involve the Intelligence services at this moment you can be sure there will be a bloody leak and I know for a fact that they will be quite happy to off load any failure on my shoulders. Just think about it; if your raids turn up nothing the Press will have field day. I... I'll be forced to resign. As for the timing, their Conference must go ahead.'

'Go ahead? I don't understand, I thought preventing your son from making a speech was a prime objective.' Fennel felt exasperated

The PM stepped closer to Fennel so that his physical presence would add weight to his words. 'If we act before the Conference the Press will jump all over it saying I have concocted a way to shut them up and my son. No,' he almost shouted, 'he can say whatever he wants and yes, there may be an initial reaction, but I can counter anything he says about me personally. I lost my wife and after that, I did well for him. I made sure he had the best education and a good job as an architect in the city. I will imply that he owes me a lot. And as for the IDM; until now it has been based on idealism but at their Conference they will be exposed to detail exactly what they are and how they will rule differently. That will give us something to attack.'

The words and finally the meaning began to seep

into Fennel's brain. 'I see, yes, that is good Prime Minister.'

Back to titles, the PM noticed. 'Now, listen up. Matheson is very good, one of the best. I had him checked out when Staniforth appointed him. I admit, he has been a bit cagey with me but I put that down to two things. First, he is a little concerned about my son being involved and was concerned for my feelings and secondly, unlike you going off half-cocked, he is very thorough. Work with him, Toby, and learn from him.'

Fennel nodded. 'Yes, I see, yes, perhaps I misjudged him. But he seemed so unwilling to speak up at our meeting.'

'Perhaps you did not give him the chance. Now, have another meeting with him and get yourself on his side. He has put together a good team, so I understand.'

'He has a team? I didn't..... .' Fennel let his words trail off.

On his way back to his office, Fennel sat in the back of his official car and offered no words to the driver. His mind was whirling from his encounter with the PM. The word 'Shit' was prominent in his thoughts. He had to arrange another meeting with Matheson and this was going to be difficult to handle; especially for his ego.

* * *

Marcus slept very well and was woken in the morning by Celia who brought him a cup of tea - with a saucer, of course.

'Cooked breakfast in thirty minutes,' she informed him and smiled as she moved to the door. She paused and looked back, 'An undisturbed night, I hope?'

Marcus smiled, 'Very quiet, thank you. Oh, Ces, there is just one more thing.'

'Yes?'

'I just wanted to say thank you for everything. I know you are the heart of this household.'

Celia blushed. 'Thank you, Marcus. I appreciate your thoughts.' She smiled, dipped her head as a way of thanking him and slid sideways out of the door.

After drinking his tea, he showered, dressed and made his way down to the kitchen where the smell of scrambled eggs and bacon assailed his senses as he entered. His uncle was already seated at the large wooden farmhouse style table and tucking into a plate full of things plastered over with a brown sauce. He waved Marcus to the table with his fork as he put aside the morning paper.

'You will be pleased to know you do not feature anywhere in the morning paper,' he informed him

Marcus sat, 'That's pleasing to know.'

'It doesn't mean they have forgotten about you. I suspect they've realised you have disappeared and are running around like headless chickens trying to find you. I lay odds it will be no later than lunchtime when someone appears at our front door.'

'Wrong,' Julia said as she entered the kitchen, 'there's a car parked at the end of the drive and if I'm not mistaken, there is a pair of binoculars trained on us right now.'

Robert cursed, 'Shit', and Celia made a suitable disapproving noise.

Julia sat at the table and reached for her coffee. 'No problem; you keep away from the windows, Marcus and after breakfast I will casually walk down to them and shoo them away.'

'Ah, the mad Rake Woman strikes again,' Robert laughed.

'No,' Julia said, 'I shall take something gooey that I can throw if they refuse to leave.'

'Ah, that shows such devotion,' Marcus laughed; 'and all for little old me.'

'Little old you, nothing,' Julia said, 'I shall enjoy myself. I shall wear my shortest skirt with black stockings and suspenders and while their eyes are popping out, I shall politely tell them to bugger off.'

'With no warning to leave?' queried Robert.

Julia thought for a moment. 'I shall open my eyes wide, bend forward to show my ample cleavage and politely ask them, in my most innocent voice, if the gentlemen would mind leaving our premises and....' She paused, 'then I'll tell them to bugger off.'

'That should do it,' Celia chimed in. 'Dressed like a whore and swearing like a trooper.'

Julia turned to face her sister. 'Perhaps you should go, dear sister, dressed like the nun you are and you can give them three Hail Mary's as they drive off.'

'Enough,' Robert interceded, 'If anyone goes to speak with them it will be me.'

'Perhaps I... ', Marcus started.

'No!' Robert cut him off. 'You keep out of sight. I shall try to convince them that you are not here.'

Later, when breakfast was finished, Robert sauntered down the drive. He saw two men seated in the front of the car and one holding a pair of binoculars which he hurriedly lowered out of sight as Robert approached. Robert casually leaned forward and peered into the car.

'I can guess why you gentlemen are here but for a lost cause, I'm afraid. Young Marcus is not here and I'm not expecting him.'

The two men looked at each other and then back to Robert. 'We had good information that he was driving up here.'

Robert turned and surveyed the drive. 'There is no car here,' he said. 'Whoever gave you that information was wrong. Let's be sensible, this is the last place he would come as it would be the first place you would look.'

'Maybe,' the man nearest said and wiped the back

of his hand across his chin. 'Perhaps we'll stay for a while in case he turns up.'

'By all means do so,' Robert said, 'would you like my daughter to bring you a cup of tea?'

The man nearest to him smiled. 'That's good of you but we have a flask and sandwiches.'

Robert nodded and began to turn away and then turned back to face them. 'I think I ought to warn you that around here there is a woman they call the Mad Rake Woman. She gets a bit aggressive with strangers.'

'I did hear something about her,' the nearest man said with a laugh. 'We'll keep a careful watch.'

Robert nodded and returned to the house.

When he entered the house, his daughters and Marcus were waiting in the hallway with eager anticipation. Robert smiled, 'I don't think they will stay too long. As I walked towards the house, I noticed the lace curtains in the lounge will stop anyone from seeing into the room so I suggest that Marcus remain in there most of the time.'

'Perhaps we can go there now,' Marcus suggested, 'one reason I came here was to ask for some advice from you.'

'Me too,' Julia volunteered.

'And I suppose I will clear the breakfast things away,' Celia mumbled and disappeared into the kitchen.

Julia took Marcus's arm and guided him into the lounge. 'Now let's all sit down and you can tell us your problem. Or are there several?'

'Do you mind Julia being part of this?' Robert enquired.

Julia immediately said, 'Of course he doesn't mind.'

Marcus sat down on the sofa. 'Not at all, some of it concerns a certain young lady and I would like input from both of you. In fact, I would like Celia to be present and give her opinion.'

'What?' Julia almost shouted before realising her raised voice. 'Sorry, I mean, does she know what is going on?'

'I have kept her up to date,' Robert said quickly. 'She deserves to know.'

'Quite right,' Marcus agreed. He got up and left the room and a moment later returned with Celia. He sat down on the sofa and patted the cushion next to him.

Before Celia could move, Julia said, 'Oh good,' and snuggled herself next to him. Celia sat on the outer cushion. Robert shook his head and sat in an armchair.

'Well, I suppose I had better kick off,' said Marcus. 'The main issues are, I have agreed to make this speech, rightly or wrongly but I am determined to do so. I thought at first that my father may or probably will, try to prevent me making the speech. I pondered this and...'

'Hold on,' Robert interrupted, 'one thing at a time. Now, I agree he may try to prevent it but the point is; how could he do so?'

There was a moment of reflection between them before Julia ventured, 'Perhaps he will concoct some sort of lie and have Marcus arrested.'

Robert grunted. 'No, that would be difficult to arrange, even for him and it would be very risky. No, I think my brother will be more subtle than that.'

'I was going to say,' Marcus began, 'he will allow me to make the speech and then he will attack. Some sort of character assassination or something.'

'Yes,' Robert concurred. 'That seems more like him. You have not finished drafting the speech yet?' he enquired of Marcus. 'Are you intending to make it a direct personal attack on him?'

Marcus smiled. 'No, I know my father too well. I have the speech well planned; I have thought deeply about it. I intend not to mention him and refer only indirectly to him but it will be implicitly obvious that he is the target. That is the difficulty I have framing the speech. I have to choose the right words.'

'Sounds sensible,' Celia concurred.

'Hmmm,' Julia smiled, 'I'm beginning to like this intrigue. It's beginning to sound like a mystery novel.'

'A mystery I must solve in the final draft of the speech,' Marcus added.

'Well, if we can help?' Robert offered.

'Oh yes,' Julia added, 'Let me help as well. You know; more hands to the pump and all that.'

'And of course, any little thing I can do,' Celia added.

'Or too many cooks,' Robert ventured. 'I advise you take some time by yourself, Marcus. They will have to be your words. Then, Julia, Celia and I can cast an eye through it and let you have our honest opinion.'

'I don't think I shall finish it here but over the next two weeks in the Safe House Sam is arranging, I can devote time and email it to you.'

'Good,' Julia said, 'and now the next point. I suspect it is about this green eyed goddess.'

Marcus looked at her and tried to smile but it didn't quite work. 'I thought you would be more interested in that point.'

'Of course I am,' Julia couldn't prevent a giggle. 'I find her intriguing and I haven't even met her. Come on, tell Auntie the problem.'

Celia stood up. 'I shall go and clear up the breakfast things. Julia is far more qualified when it comes to the sordid side of life.'

Robert stood up. 'This isn't my area either so I'll leave you two to discuss it.'

Marcus waited until they were alone and then turned to Julia. 'Before you give me your pearls of wisdom, let me explain how I have thought things through.'

'You are talking about this green eyed goddess, I presume.' Julia ventured before he could start.

'Of course; now, as I see it, if I just cut her off completely she is not a woman to be deterred and she will insist, in various ways, to keep our relationship going.'

Julia chuckled. 'Relationship.... I'm sorry; I know it is not funny.'

Marcus ignored her interruption. 'So,' he tried to ignore her, 'I then realised that being tucked away in a Safe House, she won't know how to contact me.'

'Who knows about your arrangements with a Safe House?'

'That's the good part. Sam is arranging it all and I guess his superior but I bet no one else knows.'

Julia thought for a moment. 'The problem is; what will she do when she finds you have disappeared?'

'What can she do?'

Julia prodded him with her fingertips. 'You obviously don't know a woman when she finds her hooks are slipping. I think you had better tell her. Not about the Safe House but just say you are going away for a short time to sort out your speech.'

Marcus thought for a moment. 'But how should I

tell her? Sam is coming here and driving me directly to the Safe House, I won't have a chance to see her.'

Julia tutted and shook her head. 'Seeing her is the last thing you should do. Don't even call her. Leave her a text message.' Julia thought for a moment. 'I'll draft it for you. I know how a woman's mind works; especially her type of woman. You can then send it just before this Sam comes and picks you up. And,' she added as an afterthought, 'if she rings your mobile, don't answer it.' She saw Marcus's expression. 'Do you promise?'

Marcus nodded and then reached over and hugged her. 'I know in my heart you are right.' He kissed her cheek.

* * *

On the Sunday morning, Matheson rang Sam before travelling south of the river to see him. The London streets were quiet and he parked near his house.

'Sorry again,' he apologised as Sam opened the door. 'I had to talk to you,' Sam stood aside as he entered. 'I'm getting that feeling in my water again.'

'No problem,' Sam said as he closed the door and led the way into the small front room. 'Would you like a coffee?'

Matheson declined and waited until they were

both seated. 'I expected Fennel to contact me again. I know he had a meeting with the PM who called me and told me he'd had a meeting with Fennel after he saw me. Apparently, he chewed Fennel out and told him to meet me again and get off on a better footing.'

'And did he?' Sam asked.

'No and that bothers me. I spoke with my colleagues at MI5 and MI6 but Fennel has not contacted them either. That means Fennel is biding his time and thinking which is not good. The more he thinks, the more likely he will come up with some cock-eyed plan and deliver it to me as a fait-accompli.' Matheson tugged his bottom lip which Sam noticed before only when Matheson was stressed.

'Have you spoken with Staniforth?'

Matheson shook his head. 'I'm not quite sure what the next step should be.'

Sam intertwined his fingers and studied them. 'Has he contacted the Met?'

'No, I thought of that and thought of calling their Chief Constable. What Fennel does not know is that I go a long way back and have many friends in most areas. Unfortunately I do not know the latest Head of the Met. But what Fennel has not considered, despite him being the Home Secretary, they are the police force and operate within the law unlike our friends in the Intelligence sections who, for all the right reasons, of course, occasionally stray over the line.' He coughed and gave a little laugh. 'And us of course.'

Sam chuckled, 'Well, we only bend the rules a little and not too often and only for the good of the realm.'

Matheson smiled and waved it aside. 'Enough,' he said softly, 'returning to Mr. Fennel, I don't fancy holding a raging bull by the tail. Better to put a rope through the ring in his nose.'

'What have you in mind?' Sam asked.

'I thought of having a meeting with Fennel and hinting that our focus was on Wilder and not the whole Movement.'

'What about Dolan?'

Matheson thought for a minute. 'Yes, perhaps, but only a hint of his involvement with Wilder and then we must convince him that we have plans to apprehend Dolan the next time he steps in this country.'

Sam thought for a moment. 'Enough to wet his appetite and show we have it under control.'

'Precisely,' Matheson said.

'I think you are right,' Sam said, 'you will be feeding Fennel enough to perhaps stop him doing anything rash. I think you should mention Dolan but not his relationship with Diana. He will realise that Dolan is our problem and we shall net Wilder in with him. If you mention Diana's involvement he may well conjure a complete conspiracy and decide to rush in which will complicate matters if he gets to hear anything about her relationship with Marcus.'

Matheson stood up. 'Thank you Sam, I knew a little chat with you would calm my fears. You know, working with the PM seemed hard at the time but compared with Fennel...'

Sam laughed, 'Yes, I know what you mean.'

'By the way, did you deliver Marcus to his Uncle's place?'

'Yes and I shall be picking him up Monday and taking him to our little house in the country.'

'Hopefully, with him out of the way, things will quieten down a bit.'

Sam shook his head. 'I am afraid not until we attach the rope to Fennel's nose.'

CHAPTER EIGHT
TIME ALONE

Marcus relaxed through the weekend with playing chess with his uncle, going for walks with Julia and sampling Celia's superb cooking.

On the Sunday morning, Julia coaxed him into a walk into the village, partly to get another packet of 'fags' as she called them and then to smoke them unbeknown to Celia. They walked through the village to a small stone bridge which spanned an equally small river that flowed lazily through its one arch. They paused halfway across leaning against the stone parapet and watched the river, dark even in the morning sun. 'Do you want to play Pooh Sticks?' Julia smiled broadly.

Marcus looked around. 'I see no sticks.'

Julia grimaced and flicked her cigarette into the river. 'Do you know,' Marcus said, 'that cigarette butt may float all the way down to the sea and finally choke a fish?'

'Is that how we get smoked haddock?' Julia laughed.

Marcus just shook his head. 'So,' he said, 'we have talked about my problems, what about you? You said before you were unsettled here. Have you thought more about it?'

Julia took a while to think. 'To be honest; no. Daddy is very good to me and my relationship with Celia is mainly an act. You know, a sister act. At home, everything is fine; it is just living in this small village and its lack of life. I need something else but haven't a clue what it is. Sounds stupid I know, but how can I move on? It's frustrating really.'

'I know you mentioned before about coming to live at my apartment in London but I do not think that would be an answer. Living with me would have its restrictions and finding a job that could pay your way to your own place would be hard.'

'Perhaps daddy could help me there,' she opined.

'Believe me, the price to buy or even rent in the London area would put a strain on his pocket.'

Julia pulled a face. 'I suppose I shall just have to wait for some Prince Charming to come along and whisk me off on his white charger.'

Marcus put his arm round her. 'That is not the answer and you know it.'

'Yes.' Was all she said and she stared down into the river.

It was not until the Monday morning that Robert steered Marcus to the quiet lounge after ensuring Celia and Julia were busy elsewhere.

'You may think I am a worrying old Aunt,' Robert said as they sat in facing armchairs, 'But I wanted a last word with you before you leave.'

Marcus did not respond and so Robert continued. 'I have been giving a lot of thought to the situation you are in. I have to admit that I am concerned and not just because of my brother. The Security Forces are going to great lengths to look after you and it raises the question "Why?"' Marcus still did not respond so Robert went on. 'Have you not questioned it yourself?'

Marcus shook his head slowly. 'No, quite frankly, I have not. Sam did explain that there could be certain parties who would like to stop me making the speech but not with a physical threat against me.'

'So how else would someone stop you making the speech?'

Marcus shrugged. 'I have not given it a lot of thought. I suppose I have been thinking about the special project I must complete and composing the speech. Really uncle, I think too much is being made of my speech.'

'There are a lot of people who would like to stop you making it, especially after the Press made so much about it. I have to admit without shame that I do not trust my brother and I think he may go to certain lengths to stop you. Nothing too drastic but some way of making sure you do not. I don't know what he could do but he does command a lot...'

'Uncle Robert,' Marcus interrupted, 'if I do not make that speech through.... through say an accident, he will turn the spotlight immediately on himself. I don't think, no matter how much he wants to stop me, he would risk that. Look, Sam and his colleagues are just taking precautions and as it turns out, it is the best thing I could hope for; a quiet place to complete my project and write my speech. Even my exalted father will not know where I have been hidden away.'

Robert relaxed back in his chair. 'Okay. I suppose you are right. At least you should be safe.'

Marcus got up and went over to his Uncle and put a hand on his shoulder. 'I'll be safer than you.'

Robert looked up quickly. 'Why do you say that?'

Marcus shrugged. 'Well, what with the Mad Rake Woman on the loose and your two sparring daughters, I think I will be the safer.'

Robert burst out laughing. 'I suppose you are right. But look after yourself and as I will not see you before, I know your speech will go well. I will not wish you good luck as I do not think you need it. Just speak from your heart.'

Sam picked up Marcus around noon on the Monday. He sat in the car while Marcus came out of the house closely followed by his uncle and his two daughters. After his farewells, Marcus put his cases in the back and then climbed in next to Sam who noticed Robert was closely watching him as if he wanted to say something but at the last moment decided not to.

'Off we go coachman and don't spare the horses,' Marcus said cheerfully.

Sam put the car in Drive and laughed. 'You sound very happy. Did you have a good weekend with your uncle?'

'Splendid,' said Marcus, 'and I am looking forward to some time alone. I have quite a bit of work to catch up on.'

'Well, I think you will be pleased with the place we have chosen for you and all your equipment has been delivered.'

'Then all is right with the world,' Marcus said, 'I don't suppose you have also laid on a cool beer and a hot woman?'

Sam smiled but he felt Marcus was putting on a brave face.

Sam guided the car into a narrow driveway and stopped. 'Well, this is it.'

Marcus looked at the small cottage in front of them – like something out of a Doris Day movie he once saw. It boasted a white picket fence and a trailing rose bush around the porch door.

'Looks superb,' Marcus observed, 'but where are we? I didn't see any other houses close by.'

'That is why we chose it. No close neighbours to bother you. The department bought it from me several years ago. I told you an aunt of mine left it to me in her Will but after a while, I was not using it and my boss suggested I sell it to the department as a safe house. You are not the first and will not be the last to occupy it.' Sam opened his door. 'We are about four miles from Arundel in Sussex.'

Sam helped him in with his cases. Marcus looked around – the ground floor consisted of two rooms; a lounge with a sofa and one armchair, a small table, a reasonably large television and a Welsh Dresser of dark oak against one wall which contained books on its shelves. The other room was a small kitchen which offered a cooker, sink, washing machine, a double door fridge-freezer and a coffee maker.

'There's a line out the back you can hang your washing and the iron is in a cupboard under the stairs,' Sam advised. 'There is probably enough food in the fridge and the freezer but if you run low, like milk, just give us a call. And that reminds me, here is a mobile.' He handed over a small set to Marcus. 'It has only one number, just press the call button and it will come straight through to us. Use in emergency though I do not expect that will happen or to order anything you need. Please do not use your mobile. In fact, I want you to switch it off.' He studied Marcus's face. 'I am serious. No other calls.'

Marcus nodded. 'What about my drawing equipment?'

'Up the stairs,' Sam led the way up a narrow wooden staircase. 'To the left is the bathroom with shower and here,' he opened a door to the right, 'is your bedroom. Not fancy but functional.

Marcus looked briefly into the room and noted the large bed. 'And my drawing equipment?' he queried again.

'Ah yes. That is down stairs again. I think you will like it.'

Sam led the way back down and then traversed the lounge to a far corner where he opened a door. Marcus followed him into the room.

'This is an extension to the cottage, you see it is very modern and will give you plenty of light.'

Marcus was taken aback. The room was like a glass conservatory spanning the width of the cottage and his equipment had been assembled in the middle. He walked around it; whoever had put it together knew what they were doing.

'I trust it meets, Sirs, satisfaction?' Sam chuckled, seeing Marcus smiling.

'Oh yes, Smithers. And you can tell cook to open a couple of beers.'

'As much as I would love one, I must be getting back to London,' Sam said, 'No rest for the wicked.'

Marcus retained his smile. 'And how wicked are you?' he asked.

Sam did not answer and after a brief tour to show Marcus the essential switches and remotes he departed leaving Marcus standing for a moment, surveying the lounge room. He shrugged, 'At least I shall be comfortable and well fed,' he said aloud but there came no answer.

The days that followed were surprisingly relaxing as Marcus set no timetable and worked on whatever he felt like. At times he went through the notes he had of his speech but mostly he addressed the project with the design of the house and grounds. As the drawing took on a tangible draft, he sat back and admired his creation. He knew they would be pleased and TJ would forgive him, hopefully, of the problem with the media.

No task became arduous and then he got in the habit of taking evening walks, weather permitting, and heavily wrapped in overcoat and hat he went out the back and climbed up a small hill with a copse of trees at the top. From there he could see the castle at Arundel and the River Arun winding its way passed the town. One morning, he rose early and walked into Arundel and had breakfast in a café near the castle.

The wind could be strong and biting but each time he returned to the cottage he felt exhilarated; everything seemed so far away: his father, Diana; even Sam and the Security Forces. He thought about Kate but even the memory of her faded; at least he accepted that their break up was probably for the best. They had had good times but there were also occasions when he had questioned his deeper feelings for her and the speed she left him made him realise that their relationship was more hollow than sound.

He dismissed any further thoughts and buried himself in his work.

* * *

When Sam returned to town, the next day he went to his office in the IDM Centre. It was not large or modern but two houses converted into one. Sam's office was small but handy for the library of records which occupied most of his time. He sat in his office reviewing the schedule for the forthcoming Conference when his door opened without the usual knock on the door. He looked up as Diana entered. He laid aside the papers and noted her green eyes were brighter than normal.

Diana moved to the front of his desk; her arms were straight and tense and tucked to her side. 'Where is he?' she asked.

Sam tried to smile. 'Of whom are you enquiring?'

'You know damn well who I mean,' she raised her voice and he noticed her eyes were gaining even more brightness.

Sam tried his best to look casual but he felt a tenseness tick in his neck. 'Why should I know where he is, assuming you mean Marcus?'

She leaned forward and placed her balled fists on his desk. 'I know you have hidden him away somewhere; I saw you leaving his apartment last week. Who are you, Sam?'

Sam was taken aback by her revelation but he held his face steady, not trying to give away any emotion. 'Yes, I have arranged for him to have a quiet period to finish his work on his speech and the architectural project which is, after all, his main occupation. He asked me to find him somewhere so that he could finish them both in peace; no media and all that.'

'Where is this place?' she insisted to know.

'A place left to me by an ageing aunt. It's very nice actually. I never expected her leave me anything. She was as dotty as a teapot.'

'Never mind your dotty aunt, where is it? Where have you hidden him?'

Sam felt he was back in control and there was no way he would tell her where Marcus was. 'Can't tell you,' he said simply with a smile.

She stood almost swaying with fury. 'I need to see him. The Conference is almost upon us and I need to go through his speech with him. Just to make sure it is what we want.'

'Surely it is what he wants to say. After all, they will be his words.'

'That is just where you are wrong. His words are for the IDM.'

Sam stood up slowly and moved around his desk. He was a head shorter than Diana but he did not feel at a disadvantage. 'Now look here, young lady. He has a lot going on in his head at the moment with problems with his father and the media and trying to finish this special project and he certainly does not need you to complicate matters. I shall not tell you where he is for his sake.'

Diana's mouth fell open: 'Well, fuck you!' Then she turned abruptly and left the room; not even bothering to slam the door, Sam noted.

Matheson was summoned again by Fennel and deliberately turned up fifteen minutes late but Fennel made no comment in fact, he even smiled when Matheson entered the room and waved him to a chair.

'I have been having a talk with the Prime Minister,' Fennel started. 'It seems I was not briefed fully by him in the first instance.' Fennel tried to smile but did not quite pull it off and it slipped into a grimace. 'So, let us pretend we are meeting for the first time and begin again.'

Matheson nodded but said nothing.

'As I see it,' Fennel began, 'there is, a possibility or even more, shall we say; some darker motives within the IDM. The Prime Minister has his own suspicions. Personally, I see nothing untoward with the Movement or its concept.' Matheson was surprised but kept a straight face. 'But I do think that within it, there are some who would wish to, shall we say, benefit for themselves.'

Again, Matheson merely nodded.

'I always feel that if there is corruption then it starts at the top'

Matheson immediately suppressed his thoughts that Fennel was at or near the top and he was indirectly pointing the finger at himself.

Fennel stood up and began to pace around, striking a pose that conjured deep thought but Matheson was unimpressed. 'I understand you have a team put together. That is very commendable. All with good, shall we say; professionalism.'

Matheson coughed; he was becoming impatient for Fennel to get to the point.

'My thinking is; we should focus initially on Sir Rees Lipton. A gentleman of high esteem but what better a cover to have?'

Matheson stirred; he was beginning to become agitated. 'If I may intercede, I have known Sir Rees for many years and yes, he is very much a gentleman but we did include him within the scope of our investigation. In fact, I interviewed him personally and I am assured he is not involved in anything underhanded.'

'Ah, you say that,' Fennel cut in, 'but was it sensible for you to interview a personal friend?

Would you not hear what you wanted to hear?'

Matheson dug his thumb nail into the palm of his hand; was the little shit deliberately trying to provoke him?

Fennel smiled and moved closer so that he was looking down on Matheson, 'I see you do not like my assumption but let me tell you, I have vast experience of talking to and interviewing people; many astute politicians and friends and I am always cognisant that relationships must be put aside when dealing with difficult subjects.'

Matheson had enough. 'Then let me tell you, it is my job; my profession to investigate and interview many types of people, be they friends or just suspects, and frankly, I find your assumptions not only to be wrong but offensive.' Matheson stood up.

Fennel returned to his chair and sat and his jaw dropped. One word thrust itself into his mind, 'bugger!' He knew he had pushed too far and too quickly and then recalled the advice the Prime Minister had given him, 'Work with Matheson, he's the best.'

'Perhaps,' Fennel stumbled for words. 'I did not mean anything personal. Please, please sit down.' He flapped his hands, 'Let's start again.'

'Start for a third time?' Matheson questioned. 'I have an important schedule today. That includes interviewing people whom we suspect may have important and relevant information. Please excuse me Home Secretary.' With this he turned and left the room.

Fennel seethed. He knew he had handled it badly and worse, he knew Matheson had the Prime Minister's ear. What would he report back? 'Bugger!' again became prominent in his mind.

Fennel sat for over an hour, unconscious of the time passing. Somehow, he had to regain the initiative and, most important, without Matheson and his special force. The word, 'Somehow' drummed through his brain several times. Take the initiative, he told himself; look for the weakest link.

'Aha!' he said aloud. He was sure Sir Rees was implicated in some way. Perhaps a raid on his home late one night would catch him unawares. He may net useful information and documents. Fennel leaned back in his chair; the word 'but' resonated in his brain. If a raid gleaned nothing he would have dug himself in to an even deeper hole.

Fennel reached for his telephone. 'Er... Gerald. Do you know of a Sir Rees Lipton? You do, that is good. Is there any chance you can give me his address. Yes, his main residence.' He took up a pen and made a note. 'No, that's all, thank you Gerald.' He put down the phone and relaxed back as an idea for a plan began to seep into his brain. He thought, 'I shall use Special Branch. I can't trust Matheson and his crew.' He reached for his telephone again but then hesitated. 'No, think it through first', he told himself as he replaced the phone. He sat for a while making notes before he again reached for his phone.

CHAPTER NINE
A NIGHT TO REMEMBER

Matheson was about to leave his small office when his mobile rang. He cursed quietly but he recognised the name and took the call.

'Hello John,' a friendly voice said.

'Bill Longmuir, a long time no see.'

'And now I think it is time we did see. I have a little gem for you.'

Matheson smiled to himself; he and Bill went back a long way and often opened their conversations with a little banter. 'Do you mean right now?'

'Not on the phone. Can you meet me somewhere tonight?'

'Of course; name the time and I suggest at my club. It will be quiet tonight.'

Matheson sat in a large, leather bound chair at his club and sipped a brandy. He allowed the liquid to slowly traverse his tongue and ease down his throat. The Club always boasted the finest blends of brandy. The large 'Smoking' room was quiet, an ideal place to meet his friend. As he put his glass down he looked up and saw his friend, Bill Longmuir was being led across the room by a steward. He rose with an outstretched hand.

'It is so good to see you, Bill.' As he shook Bill's

hand he looked to the steward; 'Ah, Jenkins, a drink for my friend; a single malt if my memory serves me.'

'It serves you right,' Bill smiled. The steward nodded and left.

Matheson waved his friend to the chair next to him and sat himself. 'So, what brings Special Branch to my door; after some favours?'

Bill waved it away with his hand. 'No, I am here to do you a favour.'

'I am intrigued. Come on, tell me.'

Their conversation paused when the steward returned and placed a glass with a large measure of malt whiskey on the table. Matheson nodded, 'Thank you, on my account, please.' The steward nodded and departed. Matheson waited until Longmuir had tasted the malt and then sighed with satisfaction and appreciation.

Longmuir leaned slightly to move closer to Matheson. 'You know the Home Secretary, of course?'

'Of course; what has he been up to now?'

'And you know Sir Rees Lipton?'

'Of course again; is there a link between the two of them?'

'I cannot tell you directly what is going on but I do have this terrible habit of talking to myself; aloud.'

'Of course, I fully understand,' Matheson smiled. 'A bad habit; you never know who may be listening.'

'I had a meeting with the Home Secretary this afternoon at his insistence and he has me very worried.' Longmuir paused and sipped his Malt again. 'He requested, no, virtually ordered me and Special Branch, to raid Sir Rees Lipton's residence.'

Matheson allowed the words to ease into his brain. 'And for what reason did he give?'

'A reason for national security,' Longmuir uttered the words but not hiding his contempt.

Matheson suppressed a laugh but allowed himself a smile. 'And the reason the Home Secretary gave?'

'He wasn't exactly specific although I did press him several times.'

'You do realise that he is as mad as a bull with his arse on fire.'

Longmuir shook his head. 'I know him well, I've sat in enough of his meetings to realise two things. He's over ambitious and he'll do anything to ingratiate himself with the Prime Minister. But which is the more dangerous I leave you to guess.'

'Dangerous? You class the Prime Minister with the Home Secretary?'

'Hands in the same glove; only my opinion but they both worry me.

Matheson drew a finger across his lips. 'So tell me, what has our mad Pitbull asked you to do?'

Longmuir emptied his glass. 'He wants Special Branch to raid Sir Rees Lipton's residence and search for evidence.'

'What sort of evidence are you supposed to look for?'

Longmuir shook his head: 'To look for any type of evidence of a subversive nature.'

Matheson now allowed himself a soft laugh. 'And when will all this take place?'

'Thursday night. Apparently Sir Rees will be at his country residence to do a final review for his Conference. We think that, apart from his staff, he will be alone.'

'Then I shall make sure he is not alone.'

'What have you in mind?' Longmuir asked.

'Oh, I have a few friends who I shall call and invite to Sir Rees's residence that evening.'

Longmuir began to smile. 'And who are these friends?'

'Friends who can scare off even Special Branch. Don't worry, Bill, it will all be done in the best possible taste, as the saying goes. Your team will not be implicated but it is important that this is top secret. I shall contact Sir Rees and set the plan and then I will let you know so your chaps will be aware of what to expect.' Matheson sat back and smiled. 'I suspect I shall be called to see the Home Secretary the next day. I shall look forward to seeing a Pitbull eating humble pie.'

'Of course, I have no idea what you are talking

about.' Longmuir smiled. 'That malt went down well.'

'Then I shall call the steward. By the way, do you talk in your sleep as well?'

'My wife says I snore but I've never heard it.'

Matheson arranged to see Sir Rees at his office; he was afraid that Sir Rees may raise objections and it would be easier to explain everything face to face. He was right in the fact that Sir Rees initially baulked at the idea and it took patience and insistence before Sir Rees finally agreed to Matheson's plan.

On the night, Sir Rees played the perfect host and the group of men present stood around exchanging stories and drinking the fine wines and spirits that Sir Rees provided. At eleven-o-clock precisely, there was a knock at the main door and a moment later, Jameson, Sir Rees's butler entered the room, closely followed by three men.

'These men purport to be Special Branch, or something,' he was openly distressed. 'They say they have a warrant to search these premises.'

'Well, well,' Sir Rees said as he stepped forwards. 'May I see this warrant?'

The lead figure held out a sheet of paper without a word.

Sir Rees read the document and smiled. 'Well, it all seems to be in order and signed by the Home Secretary himself.' He flapped it around as if inviting the others to read it.

'Perhaps,' he said to the lead figure, 'I should first introduce my guests.' He slowly turned and waved to each of his guests in turn. 'This is Sir Gerald Hepworth a senior court judge. And this is the Chief Constable for this area Sir Guy Rawlings and this is his Assistant Chief Constable, Dennis Quigley. Next to him is Mark Devereaux who is the French ambassador to the United Kingdom and last but by no means least, John Matheson whom you might know is Head of the Security Force.'

The lead figure said nothing for the moment and took back the warrant offered by Sir Rees. 'I think I will need to refer to my commander.' Was all he said and the three men began to withdraw from the room.

Matheson followed them to the main door where he placed his hand upon the leader's shoulder. 'Well done,' he said quietly. 'I shall let Bill Longmuir know you played your part perfectly.' The other man smiled, nodded and then departed.

Matheson returned to the main room just as Sir Rees was announcing that they should withdraw to the library where Jameson had prepared cold fare for their consumption.

It was late the next day when Bill Longmuir contacted Matheson.

'As could be expected, he blew his tank, but I kept

repeating that we could not go ahead with so many high grade witnesses.'

'And when did he come down from the ceiling?' Matheson asked with a broad smile.

'He finally but grudgingly accepted that my team had no option but to withdraw. That was neat of you to include the French Ambassador. The Home Secretary didn't want to sour French relations. By the way, how did you get the French Ambassador to agree to be present? Is there anybody you do not know?'

'Oh, a long time in the job meeting many people, you know how it is,' said Matheson.'

'No,' Longmuir said, 'it must be that silk tongue of yours. By the way, I did not mention you were there.'

Matheson waited for a call from the Home Secretary but was not surprised when it did not happen.

CHAPTER TEN
THE CONFERENCE

On the day of the conference, Marcus rose early, showered and then he dressed in a white shirt and a dark blue tie to go neatly with his blue suit. He felt good for no particular reason other than the waiting was over. He had finished his speech days before; he had walked around the lounge first reading from the script and then, he put it aside and delivered it from memory. Most important, the pauses for emphasis and he had marked his paper with a red 'P' at these points. He hoped these would be effective with his audience.

He had typed his notes in a large print as he would have his notes on a lectern and it was important that he could follow them with only brief glances. He had been taught, at university the importance of addressing your speech to every individual in the audience. Draw them all in by having them assume you are addressing them alone.

Sam arrived on time at the cottage: 'Are you ready, young man?' he greeted him.

Marcus nodded and swung his case into the open boot of the car. 'I have slept well and am ready to face the crowd. I just hope my speech is effective and appreciated'.

'I'm sure it will be,' Sam said. 'At least you will have them on your side before you start.'

Marcus got into the car. 'Do you think so?'

'I know so,' Sam said and got in the driver's seat and started the engine. 'Your father is against the IDM and the audience will be expecting you to put him down.'

'I hope they do not think this is a personal vendetta.'

Sam drove off. 'You have not seen the national papers since you have been here.' He allowed himself a little chuckle. 'Let's just say, they are on your side.'

Marcus remained quiet for a while. 'I did not mean this to be just about him,' he said quietly. 'I do believe in the IDM ideals too. My father and I have our differences and if I am honest, I do dislike him, but when I first agreed to make the speech, it was not because of my relationship with him.'

'Can I ask; do you not refer to him at all?'

Marcus cleared his throat. 'Not directly; well, not until the end and even then, I have deliberately not pointed a direct finger.'

Sam thought the young man was being obtuse but decided not to press the subject. He knew Marcus must be under enough stress and so he let it pass and concentrated on driving into Brighton.

Sam parked his car at the rear of the Conference Centre and Marcus was immediately spirited inside by a steward. 'Sir Rees did not want the Press getting to you before you made your speech,' the steward explained.

'I am in time,' Marcus asked?'

'Plenty; Philip Stringfellow is in full flow on the Economic Values of Non-party Politics. Quite a subject so I expect he will be... let's say, about another thirty minutes.'

Marcus tried to smile but inside he knew what the one half hour wait would do for him. He moved to an area of the wings that gave him a clear view of the stage and was pleased to see, along with Sir Rees and Wilder; Diana was also seated on the stage. He had been worried that she would seek him out and question him about his secret absence.

He was offered a soft drink and he chose just water and a glass was quickly delivered. He stood in the wings and listened without truly hearing Stringfellow's speech. He did notice though how the audience applauded whenever he stressed the bias of political economic strategies to suit whatever party was in Government. He listed the times and the failures of progressive Governments to tackle the essential needs of the economy and especially the people to preserve their party image but without integrity.

He did notice Stringfellow had a deep resonating voice which he knew would, through the sound system, project and enhance his speech. He began to wonder about his own voice; would it have the same effectiveness over the audience.

Someone touched his arm and he realised Stringfellow had finished and the audience were applauding and standing; giving him a great ovation. Marcus felt he was somehow shrinking and for a moment he could not move.

Sir Rees had stood and after thanking Stringfellow for his clear and deliberate exposition of the failing of the current system of government, introduced his next speaker. Marcus heard his name. He sucked in a lung full of breath and stepped slowly forward onto the stage; walk easily, he told himself; the audience became silent in expectation.

He thankfully arrived at the podium without mishap and laid out his papers. He was surprised he could see individual faces; he had thought perhaps the lighting would hide the audience. He looked around slowly, taking in each area of faces and suddenly he felt at ease. He did not know why but he could suddenly feel they were with him; they wanted to hear him. He smiled and for no reason a small portion of the audience began to applaud and this, like a wave, grew and flowed around the auditorium.

Marcus held up his arms and the audience settled. He briefly looked at his notes. 'You know,' he began, 'I have no ambition to be in politics and certainly, not to become a politician.' He paused, 'I never have, even with such a prime example within my own family. Actually, I'm not sure if that put me off.'

This caused a smattering of laughter.

'It was several months ago that I read an article in the Guardian about the IDM and it interested me enough to go along to their next open-house meeting. It was on that night that I heard people speaking about an entirely new concept, so radical that I questioned its very authenticity. I questioned its ability to change such an in-ground institution; could it survive against such time honoured and tested way of governing?'

He paused as the 'Red P' on his notes indicated. He looked up, up and beyond the audience.

'But the more I listened and the more I questioned, then I realised that here was a means to change for the better. I realised that these so-called time honoured proceedings had run their course; they were steeped in a time past; they were no longer fit for purpose.'

The audience responded with applause and a few cheered.

'I thought back a few centuries to the old days of Whigs and Tories and how politics and persuasions changed with each election. When one triumphed they deliberately unpicked what the other had tried to achieve and tried to kid the people that they were starting all over again with new ideas. This is still the same today. In the early twentieth century, there was a seismic shift in the creation of the Labour party; a party for the people. Good ideals? Unfortunately, not for long before they simply replaced the Whigs and displaced the Liberals and became embroiled in the same game of offering something different which in truth; was not so very different. What the party system of today offers is not a change for the better with each general election but simply a change of colour. Red or blue, the context is the same. What one party knits together, the next will unpick it in the name of change. There is no continuity.'

He paused again; there was a silence; he felt he had their attention.

'And then we come to more recent times. Oh yes, the pandemic, the cause of so many problems but only for the people. For some it was a time to make easy money from the uncontrolled panic of buying drugs and masks and gloves. And this was celebrated with parties by some politicians; parties at a time that the people were still recovering and in many cases, still dying.'

This occasioned thunderous applause.

'You know, we seem to be going through a period of looking backwards instead of looking forwards. The powers that be, root around to correct mistakes made by them, caused by them but never admitted at the time, by them.'

More applause started but he held up his hand and it died. He had their ear.

'I know the answer just as you do. We govern by majority and not by what every politician believes. If, just for example, in the House with 650 seats, the ruling party holds 350 seats, that means that 300 make no difference how they feel or how they vote. Why do they bother to turn up? Oh, they may wave their arms and cast themselves in ash cloth; they may shout their opposition, but they'll make no difference to the outcome. That, ladies and gentlemen, is a created redundancy.'

That occasioned more applause.

'What better than to have a system that truly represents the people of our country? What better than to have a system where every single parliamentary member is responsible to his constituents and does not have to abide by the persuasion of the few who are in a higher office and so in every vote their vote will count.'

This brought a prolonged applause. He waited for it to abate.

'What kind of system is it that needs Whips to ensure those who have doubts from their own consciences, will still vote regardless of their integrity and convictions; simply to follow the party line or perhaps be suspended? Or more truthfully, they are bullied into voting how the nameless dictate.'

There was more applause. Marcus felt he had a connection with the anonymous faces before him.

'As I said at the beginning, I have no ambition to be in politics but I am here today, to say it is a time for change. Not for a change of a party but for an ideal that will free politics from the nameless few who use the party system to satisfy their own designs and egos.'

He paused again and looked around. This was his moment, he felt their expectation. He steadied himself and in a louder voice, he proclaimed:

'To all those, and there are some, who say you cannot govern by committee, I say to them: "I would rather listen to a thousand individual voices than one autocratic, dictatorial, divisive, bullying voice who listens to no one"'.

It started as sporadic hand applause but as his meaning sunk in, it grew with vocal cheers and then they began to stand. Around the Media galleries, mouths smiled and eyes gleamed – this is what they had waited for – already minds were writing the headlines for the national newspapers.

The Prime Minister reached for the remote and switched off the television. He did not know quite what he had expected his son to say but this was damning; it would hit the headlines of the evening television and the Press would have a field day. He reached out for his telephone but changed his mind and settled back in his armchair. Something had to be done.

The Home Secretary had also watched the televised speech in his office and his reaction was similar if not more so. His face took on a red hue and a vein pulsed in his neck; his brain began to bubble from the heat of its activity. 'That stupid, little bastard,' he said in a loud voice. 'His speech was rubbish and, and....' Words failed him. He decided something had to be done.

Wilder was on the stage for the Conference, and he smiled not just at the speech but mainly from the audiences reaction. 'That should bring in more donations,' he thought as his smile became a grin. 'That boy was good.' Then he paused, 'he could be useful in the future. He could be used to keep the pot boiling.' Then he allowed his mind to progress deeper, darker. 'I could use him....'

Later that evening though, while Wilder sipped his whiskey and pondered the effect all this would have, his thoughts turned again to a darker side. 'After a speech like that; so obviously aimed at his father, what if something was to happen? Who would be suspected? It would be a time for reflection and deflection. For sure, the PM would be in the sights of the Media and less attention to the activities in the IDM.'

Marcus had turned briefly and nodded to Sir Rees Lipton who was on his feet and applauding him. Marcus smiled to him and then to Diana who was also applauding vigorously. He noticed Wilder was clapping but more slowly and softly. He looked briefly to the standing audience and waved and then left the stage. Sam was waiting for him, his face in a broad grin, looking even more like a chip monk.

'Well done, my boy,' Sam said clapping his shoulder, 'Come, I have the car ready to leave before the Press has a chance to get to you.'

Sam drove with his eye on the mirror for any followers and took several roads in a round way of getting to the cottage. He pulled up and cut the engine. 'You can stay here for as long as you like,' Sam said, 'I would think that in a few days, things will quieten down.'

Marcus shook his head. 'I think not, I'm afraid. I did not quite expect that reception. The Press will wait to spring as soon as I appear again.'

After Sam had left, Marcus roamed around the cottage; he felt an elation that he had accomplished his speech in front of thousands and the television and it had been received with a standing ovation. But! The word halted his pacing; what now?

He went into the back room with his drawing equipment and took out the plans for his project. That was completed and if he were honest, it gave him more satisfaction than making the speech. As far as he was concerned, it was over and just a part of his past. His future was sure. He went back into the living room and lifted the telephone. He dialled a number and the line purred for a moment before a female voice answered. It was T J's secretary.

'It's Marcus here.'

'Oh, I am surprised but pleasantly so. I saw your speech on television. It was so very good. I suppose you want to speak to T J?'

'Yes please Helen and thank you.'

'Putting you through,' Helen said.

'Yes my boy. Must say what a cracking speech you made. That should raise a few hackles.'

'Thank you T J but the reason I am calling is to say I have finished the project. I have all the drawings with me.'

'You have, that's splendid. Now let me think; Lakeland is back in the States but I shall call him and let him know. He will either arrange to come on over or even invite you to stay on his...' he paused, 'his ranch. Goodness knows what that is like.'

Marcus smiled. 'Whatever he wants I will be happy to oblige. Just make sure his wife is there too.'

'Yes, quite,' TJ uttered, 'now the point is, I suspect that you will be the centre of attention for the media for a while so I suggest you keep yourself tucked away for a while.'

'You mean, not come into the office?'

'Yes, I think so; just until things die down.'

Marcus felt an empty feeling creep into his stomach. 'I was rather hoping to start work again. I have everything completed plus there are other projects on my agenda.'

'I know that, Marcus, but I think it better that we give things a little time to settle. Take a holiday away or something. These past weeks with your speech and the Lakeside project must have been a strain. Give me a call in a few weeks or even a month and we'll sort something out.'

After the call, Marcus felt a sort of dejection and rejection; obviously T J was still not happy with him becoming the centre of media attention. He made himself a mug of tea and sat on the sofa and mulled over his options. There was only one.

He would ring his Uncle Robert and ask if he could stay for a while; time unspecific.

CHAPTER ELEVEN
DARK THOUGHTS AND DARKER DEEDS

He rang his uncle Robert and asked if he could stay for a while. Robert naturally agreed whole heartedly and so Marcus packed his things and called for a taxi which took him to the Arundel railway station. At Brighton he changed to a train to London and eventually caught a taxi to his apartment. He looked around the street but saw nobody who looked like they were from the Media and he walked to the rear of the building where he entered and climbed the stairs to his apartment.

Inside he unpacked, put his dirty clothing in the washing machine and set it going, and then had a shower and after that, settled down, again with a mug of tea; his favourite way of relaxing. Then he rang Sam.

'I'm at my flat,' he told Sam.

There was a long pause before Sam asked, 'And why are you there?'

'I guess I have just got fed up with being alone and hiding away.'

There was another pause. 'Are you saying you are prepared for the Press? You must realise that you are still very hot on their agenda.'

'I know, I know,' Marcus said, 'but I couldn't stand more time locked away on my own.'

'Are you on your own now,' Sam's voice carried a little sarcasm.

'I suppose but not for long. I have decided to go to my Uncle Robert's and stay with him for a while.'

'I cannot stop you,' Sam said, 'but I do not think it very wise. We are worried there may be others, apart from the Press who have certain designs on you.'

Marcus thought for a moment. 'Are you hinting that my father may do something? He is the Prime Minister, you know.'

Sam felt a growing exasperation. 'Of course not but we think there are others who may.... who may try to exploit your relationship with your father.'

'Sam, I'm not experienced with your world but I do not think that because I have made a speech for the IDM that someone will want to exploit my relationship with my father.'

'Maybe so,' Sam sounded tired, 'but if you are determined to stay with your uncle for a while, I think it prudent that I allocate someone to keep a watch. Perhaps your uncle could arrange for one of our people to stay with you.'

Marcus spoke quickly. 'Certainly not; that would deliberately bring my uncle and his daughters into this.... this circle of make-believe.'

Sam spoke quietly. 'This is not make-believe, Marcus. We have concerns that someone may wish to take some sort of revenge upon your person because of what you said.'

'Concerns or do you have evidence?' Marcus asked, feeling hotter.

'Concerns,' Sam affirmed, 'but deep concerns.'

'Tomorrow I shall be driving down to my uncle's place to stay with him and his daughters. I do not know for how long but I am going there to get away from everything. Everything,' he emphasised.

Sam would have cursed at that moment if he were a cursing man but after a pause he said in a soft voice, 'Alright, Marcus, you do what you think right but pardon me if I offer you some advice, keep a watchful eye and if you see anyone you do not recognise who seems to be taking an interest in you or your uncle, especially if they call at his house, then please ring me immediately.'

Marcus calmed down at Sam's quiet words. 'Alright, Sam, I promise I will. And Sam, I'm sorry I am being a pain in the arse.'

'No problem,' Sam smiled, 'I have a suitable ointment.'

The next day, Marcus packed again and went down to his car. He looked around but as it was just gone 5 am he was not surprised to see no one. He drove out of the forecourt and headed west.

He made his way to the M4 motorway and then cruised at an easy 60 miles per hour. He was in no hurry and slowly to the west; the sky began to lighten as the day dawned. He felt good; he was leaving behind the momentous last few weeks and he wanted to indulge and immerse himself in his uncle's hospitality and Celia's cooking. As for Julia, well, he would have to be careful but firm with her.

He drove slowly up the gravelled driveway and stopped and at that moment, the front door opened and all three came out together. As he exited his car, they each came forward and hugged him. His uncle Robert was the last and he stood back after his hug and stared at him.

'Well, no battle scars. We all watched. A marvellous speech and well presented.'

'Beautifully given,' Julia emphasised.

'I so enjoyed it,' Celia added. 'I was proud of you.'

Marcus was lost for words for a second. 'Well, thank you all. I must say, in front of all those people, I surprised myself.'

'Enough,' Robert said. 'Come on, it's time for one of Celia's special cooked breakfast.'

Julia took his arm. 'And then you and I can walk again up the hill and you can bring me up to date with your green eyed goddess.'

Marcus laughed. 'Nothing to tell there; I have avoided her since before the conference. I felt she was trying too hard.'

'Oooh! Now that sounds worth talking about,' Julia laughed as she clung to his arm as they entered the house.

As expected, breakfast was a question and answer time and they pummelled him with questions about standing in front of so many, was he aware of the television cameras and did he remember all his words and was he nervous and.... It went on until Julia asked, 'And did the green eyed goddess give you a big hug and kiss afterwards?'

Marcus ignored her question and finally, although his eggs and bacon had become cold with the conversation, he finished his breakfast and then rose and said he wanted to unpack, have a quick shower and then he would be ready for the walk up the hill.

As they climbed over the stile, Marcus avoided Julia's attempt to show off her legs again and taking her arm, they walked up beside the woods to the top of the hill. There, as he expected, she lit a cigarette and let the wind carry away her exhaled smoke. It was cold on the hill and a slight wind tugged at their winter coats.

'So, come one. Tell Julia all the juicy bits. I bet she cornered you one night....'

Marcus laughed. 'No, she did not at all. This friend of mine, Sam, has a cottage near Arundel and he took me there to keep me away from the Media. I did not tell Diana I was going away. By that time our relationship.... well, I was beginning to suspect she was using me.'

'Oh, in what way was she using you?'

'She kept on about the speech and how she wanted to help but after the earlier leak about me making it, well; I suspected she may have been the source.'

Julia took a last drag on the cigarette and then ground it under her heel. 'By the way, just who is that man, Sam?'

Marcus shook his head. 'He is part of the Security Service. I'm not sure exactly who he or they are. I think this country is riddled with security forces. There's the police, Special Branch and then MI5 and MI6 and then Sam's lot. I'm not sure where they all fit in.'

'But he has been assigned to look after you?' Julia asked.

'Yes and I have to admit he has been very good. He's always polite and very caring. The cottage near Arundel was very nice and he made sure it was fully stocked with food and they even moved all my drawing equipment there so that I could finish my architectural project.'

'And you finished it?'

Marcus spoke quietly. 'Yes. I have told my boss, TJ, it is ready but he feels it is too soon after the Conference and my assumed celebrity status for me to return to the office. He's put me on indefinite leave.'

'Now that is not nice,' Julia interrupted, 'despite it all, you have finished the project.'

Marcus shook his head. 'I can see his point of view. He doesn't need the Media to be all over his offices bringing him the wrong sort of publicity.' He paused for a moment. 'It makes we wonder if the speech was really worth making. I just want to get back to my normal life.'

Julia tugged his arm and snuggled closer. 'And you will. Just give it time. What's the saying? "Today's news is tomorrows history and quickly forgotten."'

'I haven't heard that one,' Marcus queried.

Julia giggled. 'I just made it up. It was good though for off the cuff.'

'Perhaps you should have made the speech.'

'So,' Julia seemed to insist on returning to the subject that interested her most, 'Is that the end of the green eyed goddess and what about Katie?'

'Diana, the green eyed goddess as you call her, is in the past. I shall sever all ties with the IDM and concentrate on my architectural career. As for Katie, well, I think she is finished with me. It was pretty final the last time we met.'

'I'm sorry,' Julia sounded genuine. 'But, a good looking man like you won't have any problem finding another pretty girl.'

'That is the furthest thing from my mind, at the moment.'

'Oh, does that include me?'

When he looked at her she was smiling. 'We both know the answer to that one.'

'Ah, so there is hope yet.'

He clasped her to him and kissed her forehead. 'We are more like brother and sister and I'm not into incest.'

She broke away from him. 'That's an awful thing to say.'

He immediately grabbed her and pulled her close. 'I'm sorry. It didn't come out as I meant. I.... you know how I feel about you. Perhaps we are too close. In relationship, I mean. I wish we were not related.'

'But we are,' she said sadly. 'But I understand. The trouble is; I always fancy men with ethics.'

'I'm not from Essex, I'm from Suthex.'

Julia punched him playfully. 'You're an ass. You know what I mean.'

They began walking again and rounded the hill.

'Have you thought any more about what you are going to do? With your career, I mean?'

She sighed, 'No. I suppose I shall let life drift and see what comes along.'

'That doesn't sound like you.'

'Sometimes I think one should not force life to be what you want it to be. I believe in Kismet. Let's see what comes around.'

Marcus took her hand and they paused to look out at the village below them. 'Whatever it is, think carefully before you commit.'

'Oh, such wise words from one so young,' she stifled a giggle.

'But old enough to have made a speech in Brighton.' His voice became brushed with a posh pride. 'I'll have you know, I was received by thousands.'

'From the front or the rear?' she queried, hiding a smile.

Marcus grabbed her and wrestled her to the ground. 'Oh sir!' she exclaimed. 'Do you wish to take my maidenhood here on the hill?'

'A bit late for that,' he laughed and rolled to one side. 'Oh God, it is good to feel free from all.... from all the politics and... and speeches and saying things because that is what people want you to say.'

'To be your-self again, that is precisely what I want,' she said.

'And you can one day. Have patience, dear Julia.'

'Do you want to know what I want right now?' she asked.

Marcus became wary. 'Go on, what?'

Suddenly she leapt up. 'To get my cold arse off this cold ground before I become frozen.'

Mark laughed aloud and got up as well. 'So

delicately put. My word, you do have a special way of expressing yourself. You leave one in no doubt what you mean.'

'Oh, one now is it. I suppose you got that from mixing with the London crowd.'

'Oh, of course; such refined people; especially those from the East End of London.'

'Clown.' Was all she uttered but she took his hand and together, feeling good, they walked back down the hill.

They slowly wound their way back through the village where Julia naturally bought her next packet of cigarettes. They met a few people who knew Julia and when introduced by her, they remarked they liked his speech on television. Each time, Marcus felt his face redden.

'You see,' he said as they began to walk up the drive to his uncle's home, 'even in a quiet village like this, people recognise me.'

'What's next?' Julia laughed as she opened the front door. 'Get me out of here I'm a Celebrity' or….'

He did not let her finish and pushed her playfully through the door.

The next few days were blissful and Marcus slowly felt the speech and the IDM and Sam were slipping away into the past. He relaxed with his uncle playing chess or going for more walks or simply, just being relaxed and lazy. On the following Friday, Celia announced she was preparing a special meal. Robert told Marcus this had to be her pork roast and apple sauce and with all the trimmings but an hour before she was to serve it; Celia entered the room where Robert and Marcus were bent once more over the chess table.

'Sorry but I have just realised that we are out of ice cream.'

'Not to worry,' Robert said, looking up from the board. 'I expect your pork roast will fill us up enough. No need for a pudding.'

Celia looked forlorn. 'But I am preparing a special dish. I need the ice cream. Can one of you pop out and get a small tub of plain vanilla?'

Robert stood reluctantly. 'I'll go'

Marcus stood also. 'No, please, I shall go. My car is in the drive.'

Robert waved him back into his chair. 'No, all the shops in the village are shut by now so I will have to go further out to the service station. They have a shop attached and will be open. Vanilla you say, Ces? Here Marcus, let me have your keys.'

Marcus gave his uncle his car keys and Robert went into the hall where he donned his thick overcoat and trilby. 'Nasty night out there,' he smiled to Celia, 'I won't be long.'

They heard the car start up and back out of the drive.

Robert drove carefully; the night was dark with a hint of a damp mist which painted his windscreen and necessitated him putting the wipers on automatic delay and wipe. He was unfamiliar with an automatic car but he liked the idea that the car made up its own mind what gear was needed. He felt the comfort of the seats and the hidden power under the bonnet. He passed through the village and over the small bridge and two miles further he saw the lights of the Service Station. He pulled in away from the pumps and went in. He had noticed the lights of another vehicle close behind him and tutted that it was too close for the visibility but the vehicle travelled passed when he pulled in.

When he had purchased the ice cream, he left and began the drive back, he again noticed in his mirror that another vehicle, again a large truck type, was behind and again, too close. He thought he would pull to one side but the small bridge was coming up so he continued on. Suddenly, just as he was approaching the bridge, the vehicle behind switched on its full beam which momentarily blinded Robert from his mirror. With a roar, the vehicle suddenly lurched forward, hit Robert's car and pushed it forward at an alarming rate.

Robert felt the steering wheel slip from his grasp as his car was forced into the stone pillar at the end of the bridge. His car bucked into the air and despite the airbag being triggered, his body was lifted up as the vehicle somersaulted through the air and into the river. He was vaguely aware of water coming in but his legs were trapped somewhere. Blackness was all forgiving as the car slowly sank upside down.

A cyclist had been slowly pedalling along the road in the opposite direction and had just crossed the bridge when the truck hit Robert's car. The cyclist fell to one side onto the grass bank as he looked back at the truck shunting the car into the bridge. He saw the car pitch over the low bridge parapet and then, the truck swerved aside and sped over the bridge. He reached into his pocket for his mobile phone and rang the Emergency Services.

Marcus and Julia were enjoying a glass of sherry when Celia entered.

'I hope father will not be much longer,' she said, her voice a little strained. 'The dinner is cooked.'

'It's a dirty night out there; he's probably just driving carefully.' Julia said. 'Would you like a sherry to calm your nerves, Ces?'

Celia just said 'No,' and left for the kitchen.

Marcus looked at his watch. 'He has been quite a while. How far is that Service Station?'

'Only about two miles passed the bridge. He's probably sitting somewhere in your car having a crafty cigar before coming home.'

'I notice that you haven't slipped out for a crafty

one' Marcus mused.

'Well, I will now, as you have mentioned it. Come on; keep me company on the veranda.'

He followed her out but kept a distance between them while she puffed fumes into the night air.

'The mist seems to be getting thicker,' Julia remarked. 'Perhaps Daddy is at the service station waiting for it to lift?'

Marcus looked at his watch. 'He's been gone over an hour. I wonder if I should get his car out and go and check he is alright.'

'I'm sure he won't be long. Besides, Ces is uptight enough without sending out a search party.'

'We'll give him another thirty minutes.' Marcus checked his watch again.

Julia shivered from the cold and flipped her cigarette out to the garden. 'Stop that or you'll be getting me worried.'

Time has an awful habit of slowing down when you watch it. At thirty minutes later, Marcus said, 'That's it. My car must have broken down or something. Where does your father keep his keys?'

As Julia led him out to the hall, Celia entered from the kitchen. 'Where is daddy?'

'I suspect my car may have broken down. Julia and I are going to take his car and look for him.' He saw a drawn look of horror on Celia's face. 'Don't worry, Ces, what could happen on a short journey like that?

We won't be long.'

As they began to drive through the village, they had to stop as several cars were queued up ahead and by the bridge, they could see several blue lights flashing.

Julia reached across and grabbed his arm. 'Marcus.'

He placed his hand on hers. 'Now, let's not jump to conclusions. I'll go up to the bridge and ask.'

Julia opened her door and got out. 'I'm coming with you.'

He sighed but got out and walked with her towards the bridge. Apart from several police cars and an ambulance, there was also a truck with a lifting arm which, at that moment, was dipping its arm into the water. Two large lamps eerily lit the scene. Many people had gathered and were being kept back by the police at a temporary barrier.

As they approached, they could see over the side of the bridge and see two men in rubber suits, swimming around and guiding the lifting arm.

Julia grabbed his arm tightly. 'Marcus, I have an awful feeling about this.'

Although he felt the same, Marcus put his arms around her and hugged her closely. 'I'm sure it will be fine.' But he did not believe his own words himself.

At last, as Time finally allowed the present to be, the lifting arm rose and revealed in its jaws, a black Volvo, upside down. Water poured from its broken windows and twisted frame.

Julia shuddered. 'That's your car.' It was an admission and a damnation as her fears were now a reality.

Marcus said nothing; what was there to say? He was close enough to see the rear number plate to confirm his fears.

'I think I had better go to the police and identify the car,' he said in a thick voice.

'No! I must come with you,' Julia said in such a way that he nodded and took her arm and led her to the barrier.

He told the constable in as few words that he could manage, that it was his car and his uncle had been driving it. The constable asked a few questions and then allowed them to cross the barrier. He called back to a sergeant who was over-seeing the operation.

Marcus told the sergeant the same and he nodded. 'We have recovered the body from the car, would you be up for identifying him?'

Marcus could only nod. Julia refused to let go of his arm as he approached an ambulance where the body, covered in a blanket, was lying on a stretcher. The Sergeant looked at Marcus who nodded and he pulled back the blanket enough to show the face of the body.

Marcus froze and Julia began to sob loudly; 'Daddy!'

The sergeant quickly recovered the face. 'We have his wallet, sir. Perhaps if you and the good lady will come over to the Incident van, we can have just a little talk.'

Inside the van was surprisingly roomy and they were sat down round a small table. The sergeant sat and produced a leather wallet.

'This was upon the... person recovered. Can you identify it?

Marcus nodded. 'Yes, it is... was my uncle's.'

'The name inside is Robert McVey. Would that mean he is related to John McVey, the Prime Minister?'

Marcus again nodded.

'And you are Robert McVey's son?'

'No,' Marcus found his voice, at last. 'I am Marcus McVey and the Prime Minister is my father.' He put his arm around Julia as he felt she was having another spasm of shivering. 'Robert McVey is my uncle and Julia's father. I am staying...' but at that moment his voice froze.

'Do you have a truck or a very large van?' the sergeant enquired.

Marcus shook his head. 'No. Why do you ask that?'

'Look sir, I can see this is very traumatic for you both. Can you just write down your address and someone will call to see you. Let's say tomorrow morning. No need to rush. Would you like someone to be with you? I can assign a young police woman.'

Marcus said no, they would find their own way.

If asked to recount their walk back to the car, manoeuvring out of the queuing traffic and driving back to their house, then neither of them would be able to remember their journey.

And yet, the trauma had not finished with them. As they entered the house, Celia was stood in the centre of the hall. Her features were strained and her eyes wide; as she saw their faces, her knees buckled and she collapsed to the floor with her hands clasped together and looked for the world that she was praying.

'Tell me,' was all she could utter.

Marcus knelt beside her and put his arms around her. Julia assumed a similar praying position in front of her and took her hands. 'Ces; it is time to be brave. Daddy has been involved in an accident at the bridge.'

'Is he hurt?' Celia asked, raising her head.

'No, he is not hurt, darling. He's gone to join mummy.'

Celia allowed the words to enter her and slowly seep into her mind. 'Was mummy waiting for him?'

'Of course she was. She has been waiting for him and now they will be together.'

'That's good,' Celia said quietly. 'She has been

waiting a long time.'

Julia stood and reached forward for her sister. Marcus stood also and helped her lift Celia to her feet. 'Come on, let's get you to bed. Would you like a hot Ovaltine?'

Celia shook her head. 'The dinner is spoilt. I had to switch everything off.'

Julia smiled across to Marcus. 'Not to worry; we can have it cold tomorrow. Come on, up to bed now.'

Marcus hung around in the hall while Julia took her sister to bed. He thought of nothing except the images at the bridge: the flashing lights, the claw lifting his car from the river, the moment the blanket was drawn back to confirm it was Robert, the police sergeant trying to be calm.

Julia quietly came down the stairs. 'She is absolutely zonked.'

He had not heard the expression before but it served well. She stepped passed him and locked the main door.

'I suppose there is nothing to do except go to bed ourselves. He did say someone would be calling in the morning,' she said.

'Perhaps by then they will have a clearer picture of what happened.'

'Marcus, can I ask you something?'

'Of course you can.'

'Can we have a cuddle tonight? I mean just for a

cuddle; honest.'

Marcus smiled. 'Of course; I could do with one myself.'

And so they passed the night in each other's arms; it was just a cuddle and they both slept better for it.

Celia entered his room in the morning with a small tray bearing two cups of tea. She did not seem surprised or perplexed when she saw the two of them in bed together.

She placed the tray on the side table and went over to the window and drew the curtains back. 'The weather has cleared a little; at least it is not raining.'

Marcus sat up and reached for his tea; he was about to offer an excuse or explanation but Celia simply walked towards the door.

'Last night when she was putting me to bed, Julia said someone from the police is coming here this morning. Did they say what time?' Celia asked.

Julia stirred and looked bleary eyed at her sister. 'No, they gave no time. How are you Ces?'

'I'm okay,' she said in a surprisingly light voice. 'I'll get breakfast prepared.'

'No cooked stuff for me,' Julia said; 'just some cereal.'

'What about you, Marcus?' Celia asked.

'Same for me,' he answered.

'Have a shower both of you and get dressed and it will be ready.' Celia smiled and left the room.

Julia sat up and looked to Marcus. 'What was all that? Is this some sort of delayed reaction?'

'The reverse of that,' Marcus suspected. 'I think your comment last night about your dad meeting your mother may be implanted in her mind and she's using that to soften the blow.'

'I hope it lasts, for her sake,' Julie reached for her tea. 'Hmmm, that tastes good. Ces could always make a strong pot. So what do you think this policeman is going to say?'

'I have no idea,' Marcus slipped out of the bed and grabbing a towel, made for the bathroom. He paused at the door. 'I'm concerned the effect it will have upon Ces if he goes through the whole accident scene.'

'Perhaps she does not need to be at his interview. After all, she was at home. We can answer any questions he may have.'

'True. Perhaps you can have a word with Ces and suggest it.'

Julia sipped her tea. 'I can only suggest but I feel she will insist she is present.'

Later, not long after eleven, a plain clothes police Inspector arrived accompanied by a uniformed young female constable. Marcus assumed rightly that her presence was deliberate to help with the two daughters if required. As expected, Celia insisted that she should be present.

'Let me introduce myself. I am Inspector Tryon and this is police constable Susan Metcalfe. Of course, you know why we are calling.'

Marcus led the way into the lounge and after they had settled in armchairs, the Inspector took out a notebook. 'First of all, can I just confirm your names and relationship to the.... deceased.' He said the last word quietly. They went through the routine and Marcus felt a sort of surreal numbness spread through him. He was sure the girls were feeling the same.

'Firstly, I have to ask why the two of you,' he nodded towards Marcus and Julia, 'were at the scene of the incident?'

Marcus coughed to take the lead. 'My uncle, Robert, had driven off in my car to go to the nearby Service Station to buy some ice cream we needed for desert after dinner. He left about seven-thirty and nearly an hour had passed so we decided to drive down there in his car to find out if he had a problem with my car. Then we reached the bridge...' He cut off suddenly.

'And why did he drive your car?' the Inspector asked.

'Mine was in the driveway. His was in the garage so it was simpler for him to take mine.'

'Why did you not get the ice cream?'

Marcus shrugged. 'My uncle insisted he go. It

wasn't important enough to argue.'

'This may sound a little strange, but did your uncle or your father,' he looked to Julie and Celia, 'have any enemies or anyone who had an argument with him recently?'

'Why are you asking that?' Marcus queried.

The Inspector put his notebook on the small table in front of him and looked at each of them in turn. 'I'm sorry to say this but we have a witness who saw a large truck, deliberately ram your uncle's car into the bridge which caused him to end up in the river.'

There was a stunned silence where all three of them grasped for words. Julia reached across and touched Celia's hand.

'Are you saying this is a murder case?' Marcus asked.

The Inspector nodded slowly. 'It would seem it may be. A cyclist had just travelled over the bridge in the opposite direction and saw the large truck turn on his full beam just before he increased speed to ram the car into the bridge. The truck then swerved wide and then raced over the bridge and disappeared through the village. It was the cyclist who rang for the emergency services.'

There followed a long silence while the three of them digested the news. To Julia and Celia it still seemed a case of a rogue driver overtaking their father's car through some form of road rage. To

Marcus it found a deeper pit. What if he were the intended victim? His car, late at night; Sam's words echoed in his mind. He looked across at Julia and Ces and decided to say nothing.

CHAPTER TWELVE
THE FINAL QUESTIONS

Matheson called Sam and asked him to call in to his office; Matheson's office was small, no trimmings and entirely functional. When he arrived, Sam sat in the chair across from his boss's desk. Matheson looked tired and Sam guessed rightly the he had been up all night after the news came through about Robert McVey's death.

'What is the latest?' Sam asked.

'I have spoken with the local Inspector. His name is Tryon. He is of a mind that it could have been a hit and run accident but it was witnessed by a cyclist and it points to a deliberate action to ram the car into a bridge. The car flipped over and ended up in the river.'

'And Robert McVey was driving it.' It was a flat statement.

'Correct but I suspect there is more to this. It was Marcus McVey's car.'

Sam pondered for a moment. 'Late at night; dark, a case whoever it was thought it was Marcus.'

'That is what I suspect. Apparently the truck was found a few miles away in a wood. It had been blown up.'

'Not just set on fire?' Sam's brow wrinkled. 'Looks

like a professional hit.'

'Quite. For some reason, someone wanted young Marcus eliminated. That opens many questions and possibilities.' Matheson settled back in his chair. 'I want you to go to the village and contact Marcus. We need to keep an eye on him and also, you can do some local research and work with this Inspector Tryon. Take Simmons with you. Check in to a local hotel.'

Sam thought for a moment. 'It doesn't all add up. I know Marcus made a speech at the IDM conference and he referred to his father but only indirectly and none of that adds up to wanting to eliminate him.'

Matheson flapped his hand. 'You are assuming it may have been arranged by the Prime Minister. I think that is very unlikely. No, I think someone associated with the IDM had another reason to kill him. His death may have been just a distraction. Anyway, we need more information. Can you leave today?'

'I'll contact Simmons and we'll get down to Mateley Hill.'

'Contact this Inspector Tryon first when you arrive. Get yourself up to date but I suggest you tread carefully; we don't want to upset the local Bobbies. He's bound to be suspicious that the Special Forces are interested.' Matheson smiled; he knew he did not have to advise Sam with such. 'Try to play it down.

You can say that we are interested because Marcus is the Prime Minister's son. Oh, and I am just on my way to New York.' Sam raised his eyebrows. 'I have a meeting with the FBI and CIA about Dolanski. Apparently they have quite a file on him so I'm going there to share information. This could be taking things in a new direction.'

Sam thought for a moment and nodded. 'Hopefully it will show Wilder is in this even deeper than we expected.'

The meeting with the Inspector seemed endless but finally Tryon stood up. 'I am very sorry about your Uncle; your father,' he corrected as he looked from Marcus to Celia and Julia. And thank you for your time.' He paused for a moment and then simply said, 'I'm sorry.' He then left with the young constable close behind him.

Marcus looked across at the girls. 'Are you alright?' he enquired.

Julia smiled, 'We shall come through it; won't we Ces?'

Celia nodded and then rose. 'I think I will take a walk in the garden.'

When they were alone, Marcus moved closer to Julia. 'We need to keep a close eye on Ces. She's too calm at the moment but behind that façade I think her mind is going over and over what has happened.'

Julia stood up. 'Yes, I know. Don't worry; I shall

keep my eye on her.'

After Julia had followed Celia into the garden, Marcus sat and forced his mind to think about their situation. The police would continue their investigation and who knows what they may uncover.

Then he thought about the funeral; that would have to be arranged at some time. He wondered what the procedure would be. There was so much to be considered; there was the matter of a Will and he had to find out who the solicitor was and he had to do something with the insurers about his car and then....

His mind trailed off; he got up and went into the kitchen and poured himself a glass of water. When he had drunk it, he looked out of the window. The weather had closed in again and rain was imminent.

Sam and Simmons had checked into a hotel in the next town, wishing not to be too present in Mateley Hill and thus becoming recognised by the locals, probably as the Press. The following morning, as arranged, they visited the local police station and were shown in to Inspector Tryon's office. It was small and cluttered and the Inspector quickly pointed out it was the only room available in the small station to use as his temporary Control Room.

'So,' the Inspector began, 'what brings a Special Force team to this neck of the woods? I assume the Prime Minister's son has something to do with it.'

Sam took the lead. 'Precisely that, Inspector; we are concerned by a possible motive behind the attack. We believe it was aimed at Marcus McVey.'

'Attack on the Prime Minister's son?' the Inspector jumped in. 'So you believe the incident was a deliberate attack not just some drunk driving recklessly.'

'Inspector, I think you have been around long enough to know this was not just an accident. I have read the full report. Robert McVey's car was deliberately rammed off the bridge. Secondly, the destruction of the truck a few miles away by using explosives, suggests this was a pre-planned attack and by a professional.'

Inspector Tryon leaned back in his creaky wooden chair. 'And to you, the Prime Minister's son fits into this how?'

'It was a dark night and quite misty. Robert McVey was dressed in an overcoat and a trilby and drove Marcus McVey's car. Someone could have thought young McVey was driving the car.'

The Inspector sucked on the end of a pencil. 'You haven't answered my question; how does the Prime Minister's son fit in to all this. Why would someone want to kill him?'

Sam nodded. 'A good question but I'm afraid I cannot answer that.'

'I see,' the Inspector said slowly. 'You're saying it

may be a case of national security.'

Sam paused looking for the right words. 'Can I be perfectly open with you? We are looking into something that is far greater than just the death of Robert McVey. I cannot tell you more at the moment but can I suggest something so that we can work together on this?'

Inspector Tryon put down the pencil and leaned forward. 'I am listening.'

'May I suggest that you and your force investigate and find whoever it was driving that truck. On our part, we shall be pursuing the people behind all this. Now, if you find the driver of the truck then that will be the crucial element to tying them in with this murder.'

The Inspector nodded. 'You want me and my force working with your Special Force to catch someone or something a lot bigger.'

Sam smiled. 'Exactly and it will not go unnoticed.'

The Inspector smiled for the first time. 'You can be sure of our full co-operation. We are currently going over the truck, or what's left of it, to try to find out where it came from and belonged to whom. We are also scanning all CCTV footage we have in our area. I will keep you informed of the results as they come in.'

'There is one more thing,' Sam said cautiously.

The Inspector smiled as if he had been expecting

something.

'This incident involves the Prime Minister's brother and his son. We know the PM did not get on with either of them; just family stuff. We think, that for the moment until we have more information about who actually caused the crash, that as far as the public are concerned, it was an accident.'

Inspector Tryon dipped his head and thought about it. 'There are some who have an idea what happened. There is the cyclist who witnessed the collision for a start. There is general talk. It's a small village.'

'I realise that,' Sam said, 'but I must rely upon you to play it down as much as you can.'

Tryon nodded. 'We'll do our best. The Media boys will be the biggest pests.'

'Aren't they always?' Sam stood and held out his hand. 'I was told you would be very co-operative.'

'Oh, who was that?'

Sam tapped his nose. 'Here is my mobile number when you want to get in touch.'

As they left, Simmons grinned. 'That was nicely handled.'

'Stop grinning and let us get over and take a look at that truck. It may offer us something that the local forensics is not seeing. The type of truck might be significant.'

'I thought it was blown to pieces?' Simmons

queried.

Sam shrugged. 'We need to see just how much. Come on, you can drive.'

Marcus worked with Julia to try and sort out everything that had to be done. They kept a close eye on Celia but she had assumed a new person: the matriarch of the household. Over the following days, she washed and cleaned and polished and prepared all their meals. In the evenings she even joined them in a game of cards or watched television with them. Most noticeable was her demeanour; she replaced her father and ran the household but with a motherly nature; suggesting things to be done and with a smile. Marcus and Julia discussed it but agreed that this was Celia's way of seeking closure and for the time being, would go along with her but at the same time, looking for any change that would indicate her attempted way of coping was beginning to show signs of crumbling.

The police said they would not immediately release the body but it should be soon and a funeral could be arranged. Julia contacted their solicitor and he duly arrived and went through the Will. Robert had it drawn up over a year before and it was very clear and straight forward. After any debts had been cleared, his whole estate was to be equally divided between his two daughters.

As soon as the police notified them Robert's body

could be released, Marcus took the responsibility to arrange with a funeral firm and then he went to the local church and discussed with the vicar about the funeral service arrangements. He did wonder if Celia's new found strength of character would hold up or if it may be the point where reality would dispel the aura of peace she had woven about herself.

Sam and Simmons had visited the site of the burnt out truck but found the forensics had been thorough but there was little to piece together. Whoever had blown up the truck had used enough explosive to blast it into small fragments. They went to the bridge and surveyed the damaged parapet and studied the road and tyre marks but that only served to give them a clear picture of the scene.

'Is there any point of us staying here?' Simmons queried.

Sam thought about it. 'I guess it does not need both of us. Unless the police find some useful CCTV footage then there is little to be gained.'

'So we return to London?'

Sam smiled. 'You go; I'm sure Matheson has plenty of work for you while he is in New York. I will stay on for a while.'

Simmons allowed himself a smile. 'You're still worried about Marcus McVey.'

'They have tried once and I am sure they may try again.'

'You are convinced he was the target.'

Sam nodded his head. 'Oh yes. We know it was not just an accident and there was no reason to kill Robert McVey. No, I am sure Marcus was the target.'

'So what are you going to do?' Simmons asked.

'I shall keep a quiet eye on his home and attend the funeral to see if I can spot anybody there who I think suspicious. Call Matheson in New York and get him up to date. Tell him what I am doing. I'm sure he will agree.'

'You haven't told him yet what you are planning to do?' Simmons was surprised.

Sam shrugged. 'He'll understand. He can always recall me.'

'I shall go back to the hotel and pack. It's a good job you insisted we came in two cars.'

Sam smiled but more to himself. 'It is always better to plan ahead.'

The day of the funeral arrived and Julia kept a special eye on her sister. The three of them hired a car to take them to the church which was situated at the end of the village and tucked snugly in a semi-circle of oaks and beech and birch trees. It was small with a square tower in grey blocks which made it unassuming but welcoming.

Julia looked around as they walked through the lynch gate. It seemed the whole village had turned out to attend and show their respects. They all kept a respectful distance until the three of them had entered the church and then they followed them in. The coffin was at the front near the altar, resting on wooden trestles. Julia took Celia's arm and guided her into the front pew.

Outside, Sam wandered quietly among the many gravestones, noting how old some of them were dated. At the same time he watched carefully as the people filed in until he was alone. He sighed, everyone seemed to know each other and no individual stood out.

Well, he thought to himself; it was worth the effort. He wandered over to the church entrance and listened to the service.

Julia noticed that Celia sang out loud and strong with the two hymns and stood upright with her chin raised. At the end of the service, they filed out and the coffin was carried out by six volunteers to the prepared grave. By request, Robert was buried next to his wife's grave. The vicar performed the final service with a suitable bass voice. After he had dropped the customary earth onto the laid coffin, the three of them took turns to do likewise.

The three of them stood alone as everyone moved away with respect.

'Daddy's with Mummy now,' Celia said quietly. She looked sideways to her sister. 'Now it is just you and me, sis.'

That was the first time she had called Julia by that name. 'Yes,' Julia put her arm around her. 'It is just you and me and I am not going anywhere.'

Celia smiled up to her and then looked to Marcus. 'And you will come and visit us?'

Marcus moved closer and put his arm around her as well. 'Of course; try to keep me away. I shall be here for a while anyway.'

'So all is well with the world,' Celia smiled.

Sam left and went to see the Inspector but he had no further news.

'I'm afraid CCTV is a bit scant around here,' the Inspector told him. 'Probably, if this guy was a professional as you think he must be, then he would have found a route in that avoided them. I have asked though, that the County police have a look at their CCTV records and see if they can spot a truck of that make driving on the M4 or other more busy local roads.'

'So you know the make?' Sam asked.

'One of our lads recognised part of the trucks front grill which was still in one piece. Don't worry, we'll keep looking.' He offered a buff folder to Sam. 'This is the reports and information we have so far. It includes my interview with the McVey's.'

'Thank you, Inspector. I shall be returning to London tomorrow. Please keep me informed of anything you find. I am very grateful for your co-operation.'

So, Sam thought to himself, a wasted journey but he had one last task to accomplish and he was not looking forward to it. The next morning he rose early and after breakfast he drove over to the McVey premises. He rang the bell and efficient in her new role, Celia answered.

'I wondered if I could have a word with Marcus?' he enquired.

Celia's eyes narrowed. 'Are you the Press?'

Sam shook his head and offered his card. She reached forward and took it and scrutinised it carefully. 'The police; but you have been here already. Do you have more questions?'

'No, I am not the police.' He nodded towards the card but at that moment, Marcus came into the hall.

'Sam? What the devil are you doing here?'

'I just wanted a quick chat. I'm on my way back to London today and I was wondering....'

'Another quick chat; is this really necessary?'

'I believe so,' Sam said quietly. 'Please, just for a few minutes.'

Marcus wavered and then indicated he should come in. He told Celia it was alright and he needed to see Sam on his own.

In the lounge, Marcus did not offer for them to sit. 'So, what is so important before you return to London?'

Sam inclined his head down; he had guessed Marcus would be obstinate and so he decided to be open and frank. 'We have been looking into the death of your uncle and we feel, in fact we are sure, that you were the intended target.'

Marcus almost sneered. 'You are saying that someone wanted to murder me?'

Sam was surprised that the Inspector had not told him. 'It was no accident and your uncle was deliberately rammed into the bridge. Look, Marcus, there is no reason why....'

'No, you look Sam. This is supposition. There is no reason anyone would want to kill me.'

'And there was no reason why somebody would want to kill your uncle. There is a reason,' Sam tried to explain but Marcus was looking heated and interrupted again.

'No! I have made the speech. I shall have nothing more to do with the IDM. I am going back to my life. I am an architect.'

'You are still the Prime Minister's son.'

'What the hell has that got to do with anything? No Sam, I am finished with all this.'

Sam persisted as calmly as he could. 'All we are asking, all I am asking, is that just for a while, you allow us to protect you. We can have someone come and stay here or the three of you can live in our cottage near Arundel.'

'No!' Marcus almost shouted. 'You are not listening. We buried my uncle yesterday and we need to be here, together, not in some remote place. How long is this going on?'

Sam shook his head. He was sure everything depended upon Dolanski arriving in London and being arrested but he could not reveal this to Marcus.

'Marcus, please, just trust me this once. I can arrange for someone to be here. Can you not at least to agree with that?'

'No, I have a responsibility for Celia and Julia and I can't allow some stranger living here. Can you imagine how they will feel if I tell them we need this guy to protect us? Protect us from what and who?'

'I am sorry,' Sam said sadly. 'I must ask you to trust me this time.'

Marcus shook his head and said quietly but firmly, 'No, Sam. Go back to London. I can look after the girls.'

Sam walked to the door and then paused and looked back. 'At least promise me that if anything, you know, a little suspicious happens; then you will contact me or the local police. You have Inspector Tryon's number?'

Marcus nodded and after one last look, Sam departed.

After he had left, Celia and Julia entered the room. They stood together like two small children approaching their father.

'Why did he want us to have protection?' Julia asked.

'You were listening?' his voice carried accusation.

'Marcus, we are not stupid. We heard that it was probably not an accident that killed father and he was possibly not the target. Why would someone want to kill you? What have you done?' Julia asked.

Marcus flapped his arms against his side in frustration; this was getting out of hand. 'It is only conjecture by the police.'

'But that man was not from the police,' Julia stated with some vigour. 'Is he Special Branch or something?' She allowed herself a little smile. 'Or is he a James Bond, although he doesn't look the part?'

This brought a little smile from Marcus when he thought of Sam and Bond. Perhaps, after all, his father was a little like Blofeld.

'Let us sit down and talk about this,' Marcus suggested. 'Perhaps, a cup of tea?' he looked to Celia.

'No,' Julia cut in. 'No tea, no sit down. Just stand there and tell us.'

Marcus smiled at her persistence. 'Alright, that man is called Sam. He works for some Special Force. It's not the police or Special branch. I don't really know where they fit in; there seem to be so many types of security forces. Anyhow, that does not matter. It all started when I told my father I was going to make a speech for the IDM at their conference.' He paused, wondering where to continue. 'For some reason, these Special Force people became involved. I suspect they may have been called in by my father but goodness knows why. From that point I am not sure what has been happening. All I know is, before the speech, Sam persuaded me to stay in this safe House for a while and then I made the speech and Sam warned me to be on my guard and then Robert, your father was killed.' He avoided the word, 'murdered'.

'They think it was you they were after.' Julia's voice was soft and she came forward and touched Marcus's arm.

'Yes,' he said simply. 'But I do not know why someone would want to target me.'

Celia stepped forward; her voice was steady and strong. 'It is because you are the Prime Minister's son.'

Marcus and Julia looked at her with some bemusement. 'Why should that matter?' asked Julia.

Celia shook her head. 'I'm not sure but your father seems to be the centre of all this and he is Prime Minister.' She paused for a moment as if gathering herself. 'What we now need to decide is what do we do now not what others want us to do.'

Julia was surprised by her sister's words; she seemed to be further changing from the quiet, subservient daughter to the matriarch of the family. 'What do you suggest, Ces?'

'Quite simple,' Celia smiled. 'The three of us stick together.'

'Of course,' Julia smiled. 'Together we can face anything.'

Marcus smiled too; TJ had given him an indefinite leave so he could stay, for the time being anyway. Over the past few days, he had been re-assessing his life. Perhaps he could finish the project for TJ and then he could find an architectural job locally near Gloucester and be with the girls more.

'Together,' he echoed.

CHAPTER TWELVE
QUESTIONS WITHOUT ANSWERS

Sam smoothed the iron along his shirt sleeve; the old wooden framed ironing board creaked and protested. He heard the doorbell chime and standing the iron on its rest; Sam went to the front door. He was surprised it was Matheson who looked tired and a little haggard; he usually looked so impeccable. Sam stood back and Matheson pushed passed him through the narrow doorway.

'Sorry to turn up unannounced,' Matheson said as he moved into the small front room. 'Oh, I have caught you in a domestic scene, I see.'

Sam followed him in. 'Just catching up on some needed ironing. So how was your trip to the other side of the pond? No tan I see.'

It was the first time that Matheson attempted a thin smile. 'It was colder in New York than it is here in London.'

Sam studied the drawn features of his colleague. 'Have you come straight from your flight?'

'Yes. I thought I would brief you before trying to unravel this damn situation with the McVey son.'

Sam noticed he did not use the name: Marcus and

assumed it was simply from his tiredness. 'Would you like a drink; a coffee or perhaps a sherry?

Matheson shook his head and slumped wearily into an armchair. Sam hesitated and then went over and switched off the iron before he sat in the facing chair. Matheson sat with his head inclined towards his chest and Sam decided to ask the opening question.

'What did you learn from our American friends?'

Matheson's head rose and some life filtered into his eyes. 'Oh, everything; I had a meeting with the Heads in the FBI and CIA. We had quite an exchange of information. They want Dolanski and they want him bad. He has been channelling drugs on a mule route up through Mexico and to the US. I told them we had been watching him and everything we knew or suspected.'

Matheson paused and Sam wanted to say something but from experience he waited. Matheson relaxed his long hands over the end of the chair arms.

'Dolanski has definitely booked a flight from Bueno Aires to London next Wednesday. I assume he will want to see Wilder and his wife Diana. We'll arrest him on arrival. At the same moment when we have him secure, we shall have teams arrest Diana Dolanski and James Wilder with warrants to search their premises. I suspect with the surprise, we should net some interesting evidence.'

Sam smiled broadly and only just stopped himself from clapping his hands. 'I'm sure we will find a lot of evidence against Wilder. There is his phone and tucked away somewhere I'm sure we'll find his laptop. Then there is Diana. I suspect that young lady may not have been quite so careful.'

'And handled right, I think we shall be able to keep the IDM clear of it.'

'That is important to you?' Sam queried.

Matheson nodded, brought his fingertips together and smiled for the first time. 'I know that Sir Rees Lipton is a genuine article. I do not want to see him and the IDM mired in the aftermath of all this.'

Sam was surprised. 'Are you an admirer of the IDM?'

Matheson lowered his hands and his smile broadened. 'Do you think I am immune from politics? Actually, I have always admired their ideals. I'm not so sure they will succeed to eradicate the old party system but I hope they give it a good try.'

Sam was about to speak but Matheson hurried on. 'Now, our immediate problem is young Marcus McVey.'

'Forgive me,' Sam interrupted, 'but should we be getting Staniforth up to date?'

'I have a meeting with him when I leave here. I was contemplating my resignation but when I mentioned it to him from New York, he just said he would somehow mislay it.'

'I'm sure he would,' Sam muttered. 'So, why are you thinking of resigning?'

Matheson shrugged. 'I think it is this case. Just stop and think about it; a Prime Minister, his son, the Home Secretary too and all the politics of the IDM, of course.' He shook his head. 'It is time for me to put my feet up. There are plenty of capable people to take over.' He paused and looked to Sam but the older man said nothing.

Matheson continued. 'As it is, Staniforth wants me to stay on, for a while at least. Our team will stay together. We shall work with the local police about the murder of Robert McVey but behind the scenes we shall pursue the real culprits who caused his death.'

'You still hold with your theory?' Sam asked.

'I do but I don't have the answer 'why' Marcus was targeted. Let us look at the facts; Robert McVey borrows Marcus's car to go to the local petrol station to buy some ice cream. He is followed back by a large truck which drives him off the road and into the wall of the bridge and the car tips over into the river, killing him. The truck drives off. Fortunately, a cyclist sees the whole thing and reports to the police. The truck is found several miles away the next day; plates missing and the truck blown to pieces.'

Matheson paused and Sam interjected. 'And the

destruction of the truck shows this was not just an accident and was a professional job. But I still have the question, why Marcus? Why would someone want to kill him? Surely this can't just be a case of vengeance?"

'That is why I am agreeing to defer my retirement; I must solve this before I leave,' Matheson said. 'Believe me, for some reason, someone wanted to eliminate Marcus. His uncle Robert was driving Marcus's car, it was dark and he was wearing an overcoat and hat. From a distance he could have been mistaken for Marcus. Now, three people come to mind and they are…'

'The PM and the Home Secretary and then there is Wilder,' Sam interjected. 'But surely, we cannot suspect the PM would actually arrange the death of his son?'

Matheson stood up and walked a small circle round to the back of his chair while he held one hand flat and tapped it with a finger.

'Firstly, he caused a lot of damage to the PM from his speech; more than the PM thought he could. The Press were all over it and it has not gone away. It seems improbable to imagine but the PM is a ruthless man and there has been no love between them. If you remember, he said one time that he wanted his son implicated.'

He hesitated, 'Those are not the words of a loving

father but one who would sacrifice anything or anyone to protect himself. But I still question, why would he eliminate his own son and what would he gain from it?'

He tapped his finger a second time. 'Secondly, there is the Home Secretary. He is nothing short of being a crazy attack dog but with an ambition to become Prime Minister. I have been trying to imagine his mind and how he thinks. If Fennel somehow arranged it all but keeps a low profile then the PM could well be implicated which is a way that Fennel could step in to replace him if the PM were forced to resign; that's the way his crazy mind would see it.'

'But it is a long way to actually organising a hit,' Sam queried. 'In the first place, he would have to know someone who could carry it out; a professional.' Sam paused in thought, 'But then, being Home Secretary, I suppose he might have the contacts.'

Matheson tapped his hand a third time. 'That brings us to Wilder. I have put him in the frame because of his dealings with Dolanski but he would not have anything against Marcus. I'm not sure if there is a connection.'

'Perhaps simply as a distraction away from his dealings with Dolanski,' Sam rubbed a finger across his lips. 'Create a political turmoil as a cover while he meets with Dolanski. We know Wilder has secreted away millions in hidden accounts for Dolanski.'

Matheson stopped and placed his hands over the back of the chair. 'That, my dear Sam, is the problem. We shall be further hampered while the local police carry out their investigation into Robert McVey's death. And of course, we must keep our own investigation of the PM, the Home Secretary and Wilder a secret until Dolanski arrives. It will not be easy.'

'Of course, if we could raid Wilder's home now, it may reveal how much he is involved in this.'

Matheson shook his head. 'Oh, was it that simple. We cannot make a move on Wilder until Dolanski arrives in this country and we arrest him. Any early move on Wilder will scare him off.'

'And now Marcus is suspicious of us and refusing to co-operate. He refused to go to a safe house even with his sister's and quite frankly, I can understand why.' Sam felt uncomfortable. 'I have not queried any actions of yours in the past but are you sure of this? I mean, how and where do we start?'

Matheson moved over towards the door. 'Frankly, I hate this delay while we wait for Dolanski to arrive but one thing is for sure, we cannot make a move until he is arrested at Heathrow. I am still inclined to think Fennel has his sordid hands in this somehow. In his position he may have found a contact so let us look into his past; before he entered politics and see what sort of life he led. Get Roberts and Simmons to do some undercover rooting around.'

He paused with a long sigh. 'I want you to do some background on Wilder as well, before his days with the IDM. If we can find the person who drove that truck, we shall net his handler.'

Sam nodded. 'That is my thinking too. We need to find the driver. My opinion is that Wilder is our man at the centre of things. He's involved with Dolanski and the finances and in my book, money is a big motivator. I have got to know him at the IDM; he's a manipulator if ever I knew one. Personally, I think he may have panicked and by eliminating Marcus, he could cause a distraction.'

Matheson nodded. 'I concur; he could be my main suspect too. Do a full background check and find any computer records on him or where he has been involved. Make sure you are part of the raid on his place and get any documents and his computer.'

'I will,' Sam agreed. 'I can also root around at the IDM offices on the pretext of looking something up. By the way, I have asked Inspector Tryon leading the local investigation, to play it down and tell everyone that at the moment they are classing it as an accident.'

'That's a good move. It may mean whoever was responsible may feel the heat is off for the moment and may make a mistake.' Matheson then looked serious, 'There is of course one other matter.'

Sam felt sad as he guessed what that might be. 'You mean Marcus.'

Matheson nodded. 'If, as we suspect, he was the original target then he or they may try again.'

'Then it is even more imperative that we find out who was behind the death of Robert McVey.'

'Quite so,' Matheson said quietly. 'Although Marcus gave you a rough time and told you he did not want us anywhere near him or the two girls, I feel we must keep a watch on them. Can you arrange that? I know it puts our small group under pressure.'

'I have someone else in mind,' Sam said, 'I am sure he will be more than happy to help. I'll contact him; your friend, Bill Longmuir.'

Matheson nodded agreement. 'This will be my last case and I intend to succeed.' Matheson paused before looking at Sam intently. 'Dealing with the Prime Minister and the Home Secretary could pose some serious problems. Are you prepared to go the distance with me? I shall not think any the less of you if you decline. We go back too far.'

Sam stood up; he knew the answer without giving it thought. 'I shall be with you.' He paused before adding; 'All the way. Actually,' he smiled, 'I think I may have decided to retire too. It has been a long career but now is a good time to call it quits.'

Matheson sighed again with tiredness. 'I am off to see Staniforth at his request. I think that he is getting nervous that the PM or Home Secretary may be involved somehow.'

Matheson drove over to the street with Victorian fronted houses and stopped outside Staniforth's house. He rubbed a hand over his eyes and then got out of his car and approached the main door. It opened as he neared and Staniforth smiled and welcomed him in.

'I know you must be tired from your flight, John but I need an update from you.' He led the way into his study and waved Matheson to a chair and seated himself behind his desk. 'Even I have a boss above me and he has a boss and so on.'

'And is the final boss the Prime Minister?' Matheson asked.

'Good Lord no,' Staniforth allowed himself a little chuckle. 'He's just a politician. Now, I have the gist of what has been happening but I want you to tell me. I need to know everything you do know and what you do not know. That way I can decide what to do next.'

Matheson paused while he composed himself; then he spoke slowly and precisely and in time order of what had been happening from the time Marcus joined the IDM and agreed to make the speech. He left nothing out, even admitting that he had recorded conversations with the PM.

Staniforth did not interrupt with any questions; in fact he did not move except for an occasional tap of his middle finger on his desk at some point he obviously thought of significance. His heavy brows hid his eyes and Matheson felt he could have been talking to a puppet but he knew every word he spoke was being consumed, noted and filed in Staniforth's brain. The man was famous for his logical thinking and his capacity for digesting and remembering everything.

'And that,' Matheson concluded, 'is where we are now. We have possibly three suspects for a murder and a known drug dealer who unsuspectingly, will be arriving in our clutches next week. It is then and only then, that we can move on Wilder and Diana Dolanski.'

Staniforth stirred for the first time and looked up, revealing his eyes. 'Thank you, John. That was very precise and informative. I see the dilemma. One thing, I think we should increase the protection for Marcus McVey.'

Matheson noted his use of the word 'we' which meant that Staniforth was fully behind him. 'I have a friend in Special Branch, Bill Longmuir, and he has agreed to put a couple of men at my disposal but as Marcus has refused further help, they will have to keep a low profile.'

Staniforth coughed to clear his throat. 'I know Bill, good chap. Not so sure about involving Special Branch but I suppose it cannot be helped.' He laughed a little. 'It was me, after all, who limited your resources.'

'To be fair,' Matheson added, 'we did not know at that time how complicated this has turned out.'

'I suppose not. So, next steps! You arrest Dolanski when he lands at Heathrow and then search Wilder and this Diana Dolanski's residences. In the meantime, you work with the local police and try to find more evidence of who committed the murder of Robert McVey.' He looked up for confirmation.

Matheson nodded. 'Unfortunately we cannot move until we apprehend Dolanski. It calls for patience, I'm afraid but mine is wearing a bit thin.'

Staniforth shrugged. 'Patience is only whatever the idiots say it is. Personally, I have little, especially at a time like this. Look, let's put a little pressure on the PM.' He held up his hand to prevent Matheson from interrupting. 'Let me explain. It is most unlikely that the PM would try to dispose of his son. That is a bit drastic in my book. He's bottom of my list; but, if you apply a little pressure on the PM, then that could have some side effects. For a start, you said he dropped everything on the Home Secretary's lap. He may go after him with a little head banging session if you hint he may be involved. He's known for that to cover his own arse. It may flush out the Home Secretary to do something rash.'

Matheson smiled. 'I think you may have it, sir. I could arrange to meet the PM to discuss the death of his brother. I will emphasise that we think he was murdered and perhaps, mistakenly for the PM's son. That should shake him up a bit. He may, as you suggest, then go for the Home Secretary. If he does, then it is quite likely the Home Secretary's pit bull thinking may cause him make a mistake.' But Matheson was thinking it could be come-uppance time for the little shit. 'There's a few if's in there but it is worth a try.'

'Good,' Staniforth stood up, indicating their meeting was concluded. 'Keep me informed. Oh, and by the way, no more thoughts of retiring, eh?'

Matheson just smiled but said nothing.

* * *

Matheson rang the Prime Minister and requested they met to discuss the latest situation. The PM at first demurred, saying he had many commitments but when Matheson said it was about the PM's brother, the PM paused and thought and then agreed to meet that night. Matheson insisted it should be sooner, like now; and finally the PM agreed.

The PM suggested Matheson come to Downing

Street; he would be an unknown and not cause a stir with any Press or TV present and even if it was queried, he could pass Matheson off as a senior policeman following up on the death of his brother. The PM smiled to himself; that was true, in a certain way.

Matheson was shown in to the PM's room and was waved to a chair in front of the PM's desk.

'Well?' the PM asked without any welcoming words.

Matheson settled himself; he had worked out his agenda in advance and slowly took off his gloves while he looked without blinking, at the Prime Minister.

'We have investigated the death of your brother and conclude, most definitely,' he paused for effect, 'that he was murdered.'

He watched the PM carefully and saw no movement except the PM's eyes appeared, just for a second or two, to narrow.

'Are you sure?' the PM asked.

'I said we have concluded most definitely that he was murdered. He was deliberately forced off the bridge into the river.' Matheson spoke deliberately and precisely, wanting his words to strike home. Again he watched for the PM's reaction.

The Prime Minister shook his head, a demonstration, real or otherwise, of his shock.

'We also have evidence that your brother may not have been the target.'

The PM's head snapped up. 'What?'

'It could have been a case of mistaken identity.'

The Prime Minister eased down in his chair and clasped his hands together across his stomach. 'Well? Who? Come on, man.'

Matheson thought, 'Time for cat and mouse.' He waited a moment and then asked, 'Who do you think? Who was staying with your brother?'

The Prime Minister's eyes slid from side to side as if he was searching for an answer. 'I have no idea.'

'Not your son?'

'What? I had no idea where he was. I did not know he was staying with Robert.'

Matheson listened to every word and measured every intonation. 'Do you know why he would be with your brother?'

The Prime Minister stood up and came round the desk so that he was looking down at Matheson. 'Is this why you are here? Do you suspect…. good God! Do you think I would murder my own son?'

Matheson stood also; he was a lot taller than the PM and spoke quietly. 'I came here merely to inform you of the latest situation before the Media get wind of it.'

The PM backed off and took a few steps away. 'Yes. Yes, of course. I'm sorry; it is just a bit of a shock. I was told it was an accident.'

'That is how it was supposed to look. I am sorry about your brother.'

The Prime Minister shook his head as if to clear his mind. 'And you think my son may have been the target, but why?'

Matheson shrugged, suggesting innocence. 'We can see no reason why your brother could be the target and he was driving your son's car. Your son, on the other hand, has been prominent lately.'

Matheson said no more for a moment, and watched the PM carefully. 'Has the Home Secretary said anything about this case?' Matheson asked quietly.

The Prime Minister's head snapped up again. 'Fennel, why do you ask that?'

Matheson shrugged. 'He is the Home Secretary; I assumed he would know. He should have been briefed. I know you work closely together and I wondered if you had discussed the matter of your brother's death.'

'No, we had not.' The Prime Minister walked around his desk and sat down. He sat for a moment with his head down before suddenly looking up. 'Be honest with me man, do you suspect Fennel to be involved somehow?'

'I have no immediate evidence but you did pass control over to Fennel. You remember, you instructed me to deal only with the Home Secretary.'

'True,' the PM said slowly.

When Matheson left a short while later, he smiled to himself; the seed had been sown.

The Prime Minister remained sitting at his desk but within a minute, he was standing again. He rubbed his hand over his chin as he wandered over to the window. The sky was grey with a threat of rain. His mind was singular. 'What could Fennel have to do with this?'

* * *

Later that day, after Matheson had left him, Sam had finished his ironing, put everything away and wandered into the kitchen and made himself a large mug of cocoa.

He sipped the strong liquid with his thoughts still whirling round his mind. There was no answer; not at the moment anyway but he knew they were within touching distance. There was only one remedy to unravel the knots and allow the cells buzzing round his mind to settle and then he would line up everything, the way he always did with a puzzle.

He entered his back room and turned on the centre lights at half power to give an early evening ambience and switched on the railway controller. He sat down and surveyed the scene and set the Duchess

Mail train into action at half speed. He had done this so many times but his enthusiasm never faltered. She pulled through the station and with the familiar click-clack over the rails, rounded the bend towards the viaduct around the back.

Once more he looked over to the station: people were waiting on the platform for the green Southern train to depart; a porter pushed a trolley with the luggage cases for a woman who followed close behind; some sat on benches to one side, others looked into a book-stall.

His eyes traced over to a woman with two young girls stood by a vending machine and waited for her daughters to choose chocolate or savoury treats. His gaze took in the cars waiting at the level crossing and then followed the wooden fence by the tracks and across to the village green where some children were playing between the trees while two people sat on a bench.

Across the road, a red and white bus was about to turn the corner towards a bus stop where a queue of people waited. Others peered into the shop windows wondering what to buy and an old woman followed her dog on a lead; a young couple ambled along, arm in arm. Over to the far right at the shunting yard some railway trucks were hitched to a small, black shunting engine and waited patiently for loading; a lorry was backed up to the loading bay and two men were moving crates from the back of the lorry.

The Duchess Mail train came through the station again and then Sam set the Southern train into motion in the opposite circular direction.

The two trains quietly clacked over the rails and the points and offered a soothing sound.

He eased back in his chair and sipped his cocoa and smiled to himself; he was convinced Wilder was their man and somewhere, within this web of intrigue Dolanski was the key to unlocking the door to get to Wilder. Probably, the arrest of Dolanski and the searches of Wilder and Diana's residences would bring down the house of cards. When Wilder was in the bag and under interrogation, he guessed self-preservation would kick in and Wilder would say anything to save his own skin.

He was so sure Wilder would implicate Diana and while Sam believed she was not directly involved with the money laundering for her husband, she probably knew about it. Wilder was front and centre and with no morals. Sam was sure there was a lot to find from him.

In the back of his mind, however, he was hoping the Home Secretary would be implicated some way. To Sam, he was obnoxious and deserved to be shown up for whom he was.

He mused that it would also be far more satisfying if the Prime Minister were implicated. Matheson had told him about the recorded meetings in his car and these would be enough to force the PM to resign but that was the decision for those above him.

Even more satisfying, if they found the Home Secretary had his grubby little fingers somewhere in the pie. Maybe that was so and if the PM was forced to resign then the Home Secretary would fall also.... but dreams no longer came true at his time of life.

Retirement, he pondered upon it; perhaps and maybe; he was over sixty but what else would there be to do, except build his trains and village. He scanned his eyes around; perhaps a fence there and extend the shops over there and then he had planned more trees.

He looked up at the window and saw the sky was a darkening grey; a portent of rain, he surmised.

Then as he quietly watched the two trains navigate round the track; the tension he had felt earlier began to ease and he felt he was at home and for the time being anyway, he was in his own little world and bugger the chaotic world outside.

CHAPTER THIRTEEN
THE PRIME MINISTER AND HIS SON

Matheson stood in the Arrival Lounge at Heathrow Airport, scanning the passengers who had just landed on a flight from Bueno Aires and were now crowding round a carousel for their luggage. He looked over to the exit passage and noted two of his men were quietly standing by in case they were needed.

He noticed one figure loading two cases onto a trolley and recognised from the photograph he had of Dolanski. He waited until he had loaded his cases and then stepped over to him.

'Mister Dolanski?' Matheson asked, with a slight cockney accent.

Dolanski turned with a surprised expression.

'Yes but who are you?'

'I am Smithers. I work for Mr. Wilder and he has sent me over to pick you up and take you to your hotel.' Matheson hoped his slight cockney accent would pass for a driver in London.

'I was not expecting anyone to meet me and I am heading for my apartment not a hotel. And who is Mr. Wilder?'

Matheson smiled. 'Well, he knows you, sir. Come,'

Matheson grabbed the trolley and began walking towards the exit. 'My car is just outside.'

Dolanski hesitated and then began to follow.

As Matheson and the mystified Dolanski passed outside the Exit doors, the two men fell into step behind them.

Matheson paused by a black SUV and smiled to Dolanski. 'Now, sir, if you would just put these on.' He held up a pair of handcuffs.

Dolanski's initial reaction was to step back but he immediately collided with two men who were standing close behind him.

'Let us not make a scene,' Matheson smiled.

'Who the hell are you?' Dolanski shouted; his eyes were bright with panic.

Matheson dropped the accent. 'I am just someone who has been waiting a long while to meet with you.'

Matheson snapped the handcuffs on Dolanski's wrists. 'Now if you will just quietly get into the car, we can take you to a nice quiet room where we can have a nice cup of tea and a chat. Or would you prefer coffee? I believe you drink a lot of that in South America.'

After Dolanski was secure in the car along with Matheson's two companions, Matheson took out his mobile and dialled. 'Sam? We have him. Go ahead with the operation.'

* * *

Sam had to break into Wilder's home as he was out. He had a team of five and they set about, room by room, searching for everything and anything that was pertinent to their case.

Sam was called into the bedroom and he stopped by a wardrobe and shook his head slowly with a smile. 'He wasn't expecting visitors.'

Inside one of three wardrobes, behind hanging clothes, was a small compartment, carelessly left open. Sam reached in and took out several folders and having taken a quick look, bagged them.

'There must be a laptop somewhere,' he said and the men continued their search.

After a short while of fruitless searching, Sam said, 'Stop. Let's think. Unless he's got it with him and that is unlikely, where might he... ah!'

Sam went into the kitchen and looked around. The other men followed him. 'Now where would you not put a laptop?'

One of the men laughed, 'In the fridge?'

Sam chuckled. 'Too cold but in the washing machine one could... ah... there we are my little beauty.' Sam extracted the laptop from the front-loader machine.

'How did you guess that?' asked one of the smiling men.

'A simple deduction, my dear Watson', Sam laughed. 'He lives alone and I cannot imagine him doing the washing and ironing. Besides, there is a laundry service bill pinned to the board on the wall.'

Sam took out his mobile and dialled to his headquarters.

'Sam here, Wilder's not here. Can you arrange to pick him up? We have everything from his house.'

* * *

At Diana's apartment, they found her in and at first she played it quietly and refused to let the team in until they showed her a Search Warrant and when they did, then her temper changed.

In the team of five, there was a uniformed police woman and she shepherded the spitting Diana into the lounge and forced her to sit while the rest of the team searched the apartment.

Diana sat fuming but slowly calmed. 'What is it you are looking for?'

The police woman smiled amicably. 'Oh, anything that ties you in with your husband.

Her thoughts began to race in her head. 'What makes you think I have a husband?'

'We have just picked him up at the airport. He's just flown in from Bueno Aires. We'll take you to meet him as soon as we have finished our search.'

At this news, Diana sat quietly but her mind was still racing with questions. She knew her husband was arriving that day but why would they arrest him at the airport. She began to suspect Wilder had some hand in this.

They found no papers that linked Diana to her husband and they were only related to her work with the IDM. These were bagged anyway and then the police woman asked, 'Have you your mobile phone?'

Diana shook her head. 'I lost it a few days ago. I have been meaning to get a new one.'

The police woman noticed that as she spoke, Diana's eyes had for just a fraction, looked to the left. She followed her look and saw the mobile resting on a book and by a lamp on a table in the corner. She got up and retrieved the mobile phone.

'Well, well, that is fortunate. I have found your phone for you.' She slipped it into a plastic bag.

Diana stood, she was breathing hard and her green eyes were aflame. The police woman shook her head and tutted. 'Don't even think about it. The boys here would enjoy a tussle with you.'

Diana muttered 'bitch' under her breath but, she reasoned, she had nothing to hide; she knew little although suspected a lot.

'Alright,' Diana said, holding out her wrists.

The police woman smiled. 'I don't think there is any need for those, do you?'

Diana lowered her wrists and smiled for the first time. 'I can hardly run away in these shoes, I suppose.'

* * *

'I have been thinking,' Celia said.

Julia looked up from the newspaper she was reading and Marcus opened his eyes, he had been relaxing on the sofa and was about to enter the realms of Morpheus.

'Tomorrow we have an appointment with our solicitor and he will read us Daddy's Will.'

Julia's brow furrowed slightly. 'So?'

'Well, that is the final step,' Celia said, 'It is the start of our new lives without Daddy.'

Julia looked across at Marcus and then back to Celia. 'So what have you in mind?'

'Rather than just sit around here pretending everything is fine,' Celia explained, 'why don't the three of us just go away somewhere. I know it is the wrong season but can't we just get away for a while?'

Marcus stood up. 'Yes, I think you are right, Ces. We'll slip away without telling anybody; no Sam, no police, no Special Forces, no Media chasing us for a story.'

'And not your father,' Julia added.

Marcus smiled. 'No worry there. He will be sparing no thought for me.'

There was silence just for a moment before Julia asked, 'Does it bother you? You know, not being close to your father?'

Marcus shook his head. 'Not a bit. You do not miss something you have never had.'

'How sad,' Julia said quietly.

'Well,' Celia said with enthusiasm, 'where shall we go?'

Marcus winked to Julia, 'How about the Isle of Wight?'

'What?' Celia exclaimed. 'What's there?'

'The same as anywhere else at this time of year,' Marcus said and then after a pause added, 'and we won't need passports to get across from the mainland.'

'Splendid,' Julia clapped her hands, 'a small island we can roam around without fear of being recognised. We can use false names. I have always wanted to be a Dolores.'

'And I shall be Daniel. How's that? A Daniel, oh, to be a Daniel,' Marcus chimed.

Marcus and Julia giggled but Celia was not amused. 'And who shall I be?'

'I can think of a few names,' Julia quipped.

Marcus stepped in quickly to avoid a spat between the sisters. 'You think of one Ces.'

Celia tilted her head to one side. 'Well, how about?' She paused in thought, 'Amber.'

'That's a caution,' Julia slipped in.

'Amber sounds fine,' Marcus said quickly. 'Right, we'll have to pack after we've seen our solicitor. Oh, how long are we going for?'

'As long as we like,' Celia said with enthusiasm and the other two looked at her with surprise. 'We see our solicitor tomorrow and then we shall leave the following day. I suggest we just find a hotel when we get there. We don't want to risk phoning for a booking in case anyone has our phones tapped. We won't have anybody to phone so I suggest we leave them here. Just so nobody can trace us. Perhaps it will be better if we leave in the small hours of the morning. That is just in case anyone is watching us.'

Marcus's lips formed into smile, she really had taken on the role of the family Matriarch.

* * *

Matheson stood by his desk as his team seated them-selves. 'Right,' he started, 'we have all the players in the pot so let's go through what we have learned from their interrogations.'

'Quite a talkative bunch once we got them started,' Simpson said.

'Except Dolanski,' Matheson interjected. 'But I could tell by his facial expressions at certain points, that he realises we know a lot about him. That CIA file was useful. He was somewhat surprised by some of the information we had about his activities. By the way, a CIA agent is flying across tomorrow and I think that will unsettle Dolanski even more when he appears.'

'And Wilder has been singing like a bird,' Sam chimed in. 'He was pointing the finger at everyone else until he realised that just by knowing who to point at, it implicated him for knowing.'

'So, what do we have?' Matheson asked, not expecting an answer. 'Wilder is as guilty as sin of embezzlement and laundering money. In a day or two we shall have Dolanski sewn up in the same bag when the CIA chap arrives. I think his wife Diana was aware of some of the actions but not really guilty of involvement. That leaves just two to follow up on and they will need extra careful treatment.'

'The Prime Minister and the Home Secretary,' Sam said.

'Precisely,' Matheson leaned back against the desk. 'I think, Sam, you and I had better handle those two. I have to be honest, I am looking forward to locking horns with Fennel but the Prime Minister is another matter.'

'Do you really need me for Fennel?' Sam asked. 'I find him so distasteful.'

Matheson smiled. 'I'm afraid so. He needs questions coming at him from both sides. I don't want him to feel comfortable.' After a thought, he added, 'Perhaps I will see the PM on my own. Now, we are progressing where Dolanski and Wilder and the money is concerned, but not with who killed or who hired someone to kill Robert McVey.'

'I think we should ignore Robert McVey,' said Sam.

The others looked at him.

Matheson was the first to speak. 'Ignore a murder? A professional hit?'

'Of Robert McVey,' Sam said. 'I think that is throwing us off course. We have good reason to believe Marcus McVey was the target. Circumstances unfortunately led to his uncle being mistaken for him. The question I think we should be addressing is: who would want the Prime Minister's son killed?'

Matheson smiled at his small friend for untangling the threads of the mystery and identifying the focal point. 'You are right, Sam. My mistake, I'm afraid. I have wanted too much for the PM or Fennel to be involved somehow.'

'And so you should,' Sam said. 'Both have reasons for his demise. The PM has no love for his son and since Marcus's speech at the IDM conference, the PM has been under a lot of pressure in the House and even some ridicule from the Media, especially late night chat shows. As for the Home Secretary, I believe his ambition has warped his perspective. I think he saw the death of Marcus, especially after his speech, would point all fingers at the PM. Fennel could then grasp the opportunity to replace the PM.

He's my bet.'

There was silence from his audience while they digested Sam's analysis. Matheson finally spoke. 'You have it, Sam; I was forgetting Fennel's ambition. Of course, that is part of his attack dog nature. Right, that puts a whole new view to it. When we meet with him, we shall start quietly like a general enquiry about what we have discovered from Wilder and Dolanski about the money laundering and slowly lead him round to Robert McVey's murder. Then we shall see if we can get him to make a slip.'

A few days later, with Wilder and Dolanski wilting under continuous interrogation, enough evidence was put together. Matheson decided Diana, although aware of some activities, was not directly involved and probably not worth prosecuting. That left Fennel but before they could arrange a meeting, news came from Inspector Tryon.

* * *

The apparent hit man had been caught. He was identified as Joshua Tremaine, a man from the Gloucester area, with a record of violence and assault and a prison history who was a cheap 'gun for hire' to assault with violence for a price. He had served a ten year stretch for wounding one target but had not killed anybody to date, but that was thought due to his incompetence.

Matheson travelled down to Gloucester to meet Inspector Tryon who explained a sorry and peculiar tale.

'Let me take you through the story from the beginning of the night Tremaine committed the murder. He had been keeping the McVey house under observation for a few days mainly to look over the scene and work out a plan but not knowing if an opportunity would arise. On that particular night, while he was surveying the house luck was with him, he thought he saw Marcus McVey get in his car and drive to the local village. He followed him and waited while the 'person' went into the local garage store and then followed him back to the bridge and rammed him through the parapet. He then drove off to some woods where he had left his car, set an explosive device and blew the truck to pieces.'

'But how do you know this?' Matheson queried.

Tryon smiled. 'He had never used explosives before and he used too much. When the truck blew up, he was too close and suffered multiple shrapnel wounds and severe burns.'

'Some hit man,' Matheson smiled back.

'Well, eventually, he had recovered enough to get in his car and drive to the nearest hospital. He told them he had had an accident with an old oil stove at home. Fortunately, the senior doctor at the hospital was suspicious because of the wounds and burns and decided to phone our local station.'

'And is Tremaine still at the hospital?' Matheson enquired.

Tryon sighed. 'Yes, but he is in a bad way. The doctor said it was fifty-fifty he would survive the night. The doctor said he had been rambling in his agony. That's how he knew he should contact the police.'

'Then we must go and see him,' Matheson said.

'He may not last. He is in a terrible state. I am surprised he managed to drive his car. I did question him but he slips in and out of consciousness. I only got bits and pieces which I've told you.'

'Did he say who hired him?' Matheson queried.

'No,' Tryon said, a little dejected. 'As I said, he rambled but avoided the one question about who hired him. I didn't like to press him too far.'

Matheson was on his feet. 'Forget any sympathy for him. I need him to talk.'

Outside the small ward, the doctor barred the way into the room. 'He is in no state to answer questions,' he insisted.

Matheson took out his card. 'This is a matter of national security,' he lied. 'At least let me try to talk with him.'

The doctor hesitated and then stepped back, 'Alright but only for five minutes.' And he walked off down the corridor.

Matheson and Tryon entered and went over to

the bed. The sight which met them made them both hesitate. The whole of Tremaine's left face was horribly burned and he only had one eye left. His body was uncovered and was equally horrendous with wounds where shrapnel had been removed and more burn marks down his body.

'Good God,' Tryon muttered. 'How has he survived this long?'

Matheson was less affected and showed no sympathy. 'Tremaine,' he hissed. 'Can you hear me?'

Tremaine opened his one eye but made no sound, his breath was rasping through his disfigured lips.

'Who hired you?' Matheson asked. There was no response and Matheson repeated the question several times. Tremaine's one eye focussed on Matheson but he refused to speak.

Matheson looked to Tryon and asked, 'Would you like to look away?'

Tryon's brow furrowed. 'What?'

Matheson shook his head; he knew he had little time left. He reached down between Tremaine's legs and grasped his balls. He began to squeeze, gently at first. 'Who hired you?'

Tryon stepped forward. 'John!'

Matheson waved him away impatiently with his other hand. 'This is the only chance we may get.'

Tryon reluctantly stepped back and turned away.

Matheson applied more pressure and Tremaine

opened his mouth and gasped and made an agonised gurgling sound; his one eye began to bulge.

'Who was it?' Matheson demanded again.

Matheson applied more pressure and suddenly Tremaine screamed one word, 'Fennel!'

Matheson let go and stood back. Tryon turned and looked at him. 'Is this how you boys conduct yourselves?'

'I got Fennel's name; that is what is important.'

At that moment the doctor broke into the room and went over to the patient. He examined him for a moment and then looked back to Matheson. 'I don't know what you did but it has finished him. I shall have to report this incident.' He looked to Tryon who just shrugged.

'He suddenly convulsed and screamed and that was it,' Tryon said flatly.

He looked to Matheson who similarly shrugged. 'I would say it was a mercy considering how badly wounded he was. A pity he did not talk.' Matheson looked to the bedside table and noticed the mobile phone which he picked up and put in his pocket.

Outside they went over to Tryon's car. 'Don't give me any shit about the end justifying the means.'

Matheson said nothing; there was nothing to say. It only strengthened his resolve to retire and very soon.

* * *

Two days later, Matheson and Sam met with Fennel at his office. He looked different; instead of the usual blustering figure his face was puffy and his eyes were flecked with red and betrayed tiredness; perhaps also drinking. Matheson suspected he had also been through a session with the Prime Minister. He did not get up from his seat when they entered but sat silently while they seated themselves.

'Well,' he said when they did not speak. 'I have read the reports, so you have gathered up the ringleaders. I suspect that may be the end of the IDM as an effective movement.'

'Not at all,' Matheson said. 'So far, we have proof that Wilder and Dolanski were operating a drugs and money-laundering operation. We know this was between them and in no way implicates the IDM.' He paused to see Fennel's reaction and was pleased to see Fennel straighten in his chair and lean forward.

'But there was so much more to it,' Fennel said.

'Such as,' queried Sam? 'What more is there? Do you know something we do not?'

Fennel looked briefly at Sam and then to Matheson. 'I mean, how could such an operation, with the Treasurer of the IDM, not implicate the whole movement?'

'Quite simple,' Matheson cut in. 'Wilder was simply a contact for Dolanski and....'

Fennel cut in. 'And Dolanski was married to that

Diana who happened to be Head of Administration for the IDM. What more proof could you need to implicate the three of them?'

Sam took his turn. 'We have interviewed her and know she was not involved. This was simply an operation between Wilder and Dolanski. We have documents, laptops and phones from all three. I know you would like the IDM to be involved but it quite simply was not.'

Fennel looked to Sam, his face was slowly colouring a shade of red. 'So why are you here to see me?' he asked.

Matheson coughed. 'There is the matter of Marcus McVey. We have evidence that he was the target of a hitman, not his uncle.'

This caught Fennel off guard and he sat back in his chair and pressed a button on his desk. 'Can we have some coffee?' he spoke into a voice-box.

Fennel sat quietly for a moment as if waiting for the coffee but Matheson took the lead. 'You see, the hit man, a certain Joshua Tremaine, was not, shall we say, very good at his job.'

Fennel said nothing but the name drained his facial features.

Sam continued the conversation. 'Tremaine mistakenly killed the wrong person, namely, Robert McVey, and then, trying to hide the evidence, blew himself up.' Sam smiled, 'whoever hired him, hired the wrong man for the job.'

'So how do you know all this about Marcus McVey being the target if this man was killed?' Fennel queried.

'Oh, didn't I say?' Matheson smiled. 'I spoke with him in the hospital before he died.'

There was a knock at the door and then a young girl entered with a tray of coffee and cups. Matheson cursed to himself. She poured the coffee while the three men sat in silence. She looked around, smiled and decided to say nothing and departed.

Matheson continued, 'And he gave us your name before he died.'

Fennel reached over, took up his cup and sipped his coffee while he gathered himself. He sipped again before speaking. 'So you have the word of a dying man. Do you have any evidence what he said was true?'

'We have his mobile phone,' Sam said quietly. 'Lots of things get recorded on the modern phones.'

'In particular,' Matheson continued the conversation, 'recorded call numbers and sometimes, recorded messages. Surprising how careless people can be. As I said, he wasn't very good at his job.'

Fennel put down his cup and looked from Sam to Matheson. Then he looked into his lap and sighed heavily. 'I suppose you have come here with an arrest warrant.'

'Quite,' Matheson concurred.

'Tell me,' Sam asked, 'why did you target Marcus McVey?'

Fennel smiled to himself as if he had a private joke. 'After that speech he made at the IDM conference, I could see how it affected the PM. I saw for the first time that he had a vulnerable side. That; surprisingly was his relationship with his son.' He paused as though lost in thought. 'He tried to pretend he did not care but I saw through him. There were odd moments.' Fennel sipped his coffee again. 'That was some speech Marcus made. Even I admired it. I saw how the PM reacted. He was scared. Then the thought occurred to me, this was the chance to unseat the PM. He was becoming too autocratic and a bully and he was unable to see where he was taking us. He was slowly destroying everything we had set out to do. I saw the chance to finally topple him.'

'With the death of his son?' queried Sam. 'That was a high price.'

Fennel flapped his hands. 'One life but I saw the possibilities. There would be a suspicion of his involvement and the Press would have had a field day. With the PM gone, I could have taken his place and then steered back onto the true course. I would have fired the Chancellor first.' Fennel laughed at the thought of sacking McDonald.

Sam and Matheson looked to each other, their

thoughts were the same: Fennel had become unhinged.

* * *

In Matheson's office, Sam sat with some satisfaction that over the past few days, everything slotted into place and when thieves fall out, through the hope of self-preservation, they simply damn each other. Matheson entered and smiled as he sat down.

'Happy it is all over?' queried Sam.

'Not all,' Matheson said. 'I have had a meeting with Staniforth and he has finally accepted my resignation and a deserved retirement on a good pension.'

Sam laughed, 'So, you are going to join the ranks of pensioners like me.'

'You?' queried Matheson. 'I thought you had got the taste again and would be continuing.'

Sam shook his head. 'No, I have plans of my own, there's work to be done on my railway. But what will you do?'

Matheson shrugged. 'Oh, I have some ideas. I think a cruise somewhere to start with as I have been promising myself that for quite a while.'

Sam smiled. 'Somehow I cannot imagine you relaxing back on some boat deck with only the sea to look at.'

'I can,' Matheson said, 'but first, I have one more

task to do.'

'Oh, and what would that be?'

'The small matter of a meeting with the Prime Minister,' Matheson smiled at the thought. 'It will be my one last farewell gesture.'

'I wish I could come with you,' Sam uttered.

'Oh no,' Matheson said, 'this is strictly no witnesses. By the way, do you know where Marcus and the two girls have disappeared to?'

'I have not a clue,' Sam lied.

* * *

The next day, the Prime Minister agreed, surprisingly, to see Matheson. He had read the report from Staniforth and had a brief meeting with him and was pleased on two counts.

Firstly, Fennel was implicated in the death of his brother and had been arrested and besides the loss of his brother Robert; it meant that he was saved having to sack his Home Secretary. Fennel had begun to get under his skin and his continual feuding with the Chancellor was wearing him down.

The second point was that although the IDM were cleared of any involvement, he could refer from time to time in the House to the fact that the IDM Treasurer was convicted on charges of money laundering. And that, he smiled would remind the public that the IDM was not as clean as it purported.

Matheson entered the room and the PM smiled and ushered him to sit. 'Nicely wrapped up,' the PM said. 'I have had a meeting with Staniforth and the conclusion is most satisfactory.'

'Despite your son being the real target and your brother being murdered,' Matheson said quietly as he sat down.

The Prime Minister was slightly taken aback. 'Of course, I regret that part of it. May I ask why you requested this meeting?'

'I just wanted to tie up a few loose ends.'

The PM looked puzzled. 'What loose ends? I thought the case was completed.'

'Oh, the case is so far as the convictions will be determined by the courts, but I was thinking back to our meetings. In my car, remember?'

The PM looked uneasy. 'What of them?'

'Well, I remember our conversations very well. You wanted the IDM investigated.'

'That was simply a standard procedure. It was a new party or movement. We had to make sure they were strictly above board.'

'But that was not quite the truth,' Matheson said, keeping his voice low.

The Prime Minister's body language showed he was uneasy and perhaps a little angry. 'And your point is?'

'Our meetings were covert and in my car and not the usual way to request the Special Force to investigate something.'

The Prime Minister stood up and wandered round his desk so that he could look down on Matheson. 'Oh I see. You are now getting a conscience about it.'

'No, not getting one. I have disliked it from the start.'

'And now you come running to me, hoping to solve your conscience problems.'

'No. I was wondering if you had any problems with your conscience,' Matheson kept his voice at a steady, low key.

The Prime Minister straightened and returned to his seat. He put his elbows on his desk and brought his hands together and pressed his fingertips together to form a small chapel. 'So, what exactly is the problem? Is it the death of my brother that disturbs you?'

'Possibly more than his death means to you.'

The Prime Minister immediately stood again. 'I remind you who you are talking to. I shall be reporting this to Staniforth. I don't think he will take to kindly to what you are saying to me.'

Matheson stood also. 'I think Mister Staniforth fully understands my position. The plain facts are you requested a covert investigation without a legal cause and you told me that if we found anything, you wanted your son implicated and in my book, that shows a father who is more interested in his own survival rather than his son's.'

The Prime Minister exploded and stepped forward. 'You dare say that to me.'

'It is the truth and you know it.'

'I shall have you drummed out of the Service. I shall speak with Staniforth....'

Matheson smiled. 'Save yourself the effort. I have already spoken with him.'

Matheson turned and left the room. He decided to walk back to his office and all the way back he had a smile on his face. He felt good; now all the loose ends had been tied up to his satisfaction.

THE END

THE END